"I need to wind this investigation up in the next forty-eight hours, and quite frankly, you've become a distraction I can't afford."

"Is that what I am to you," Ford said, grinning.

"I'm serious. Please go home so I know you're safe."

"I can't do that." He held Hitch's gaze. "I came here to save Rachel if I could. Instead I find myself getting involved with you."

"I wouldn't say we're involved."

"Wouldn't you?" He cupped her cheek, drawing her face up to his own. "Tell me there is nothing between us and I'll walk away right now."

She parted her lips, but no words came out. He pulled her into his arms. He could feel her heart pounding in her pulse. "Last chance," he said.

TROUBLE IN BIG TIMBER

New York Times Bestselling Author

B.J. DANIELS

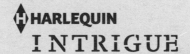

This book is dedicated to anyone still hung up on an old love.
If you saw the person again, would it ignite those old sparks?
Or would the fire have burned out? Or, would you realize that
they were never quite as amazing as you remembered?

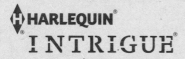

INTRIGUE

PLEASE RECYCLE
THIS PRODUCT IS RECYCLABLE

Recycling programs
for this product may
not exist in your area.

ISBN-13: 978-1-335-40176-2

Trouble in Big Timber

Copyright © 2021 by Barbara Heinlein

This edition published by arrangement with Harlequin Books S.A.

For questions and comments about the quality of this book,
please contact us at CustomerService@Harlequin.com.

Harlequin Enterprises ULC
22 Adelaide St. West, 40th Floor
Toronto, Ontario M5H 4E3, Canada
www.Harlequin.com

Printed in U.S.A.

B.J. Daniels is a *New York Times* and *USA TODAY* bestselling author. She wrote her first book after a career as an award-winning newspaper journalist and author of thirty-seven published short stories. She lives in Montana with her husband, Parker, and three springer spaniels. When not writing, she quilts, boats and plays tennis. Contact her at bjdaniels.com, on Facebook or on Twitter, @bjdanielsauthor.

Books by B.J. Daniels

Harlequin Intrigue

Cardwell Ranch: Montana Legacy

Steel Resolve
Iron Will
Ambush Before Sunrise
Double Action Deputy
Trouble in Big Timber

Whitehorse, Montana: The Clementine Sisters

Hard Rustler
Rogue Gunslinger
Rugged Defender

HQN

Montana Justice

Restless Hearts
Heartbreaker
Heart of Gold

Sterling's Montana

Stroke of Luck
Luck of the Draw
Just His Luck

Visit the Author Profile page at Harlequin.com.

CAST OF CHARACTERS

Ford Cardwell—He's at rock bottom when he gets the apparently pocket-dialed call from the woman he never forgot. He heard the whole thing—including the gunshot.

Henrietta "Hitch" Rogers—The state medical examiner suspects something is wrong the moment she's put on the case.

Rachel Westlake Collinwood—Why did she keep the abuse a secret until the day she said she was forced to kill her husband?

Humphrey Collinwood—Was he really abusing his wife? Or did she kill him in cold blood?

Sheriff Charley Cortland—The first on the scene, he could see that it was an open-and-shut case of domestic abuse gone too far.

Paul Townsend—He would have done anything for Rachel Collinwood. Had he?

Deputy Rick Birch—He'd had to come to Rachel Collinwood's rescue before.

Shyla Birch—Rachel's best friend from college knew her better than anyone, didn't she?

Chapter One

The narrow mountain road ended at the edge of a rock cliff. It wasn't as if Ford Cardwell had forgotten that. No, when he saw where he was, he knew it was why he'd taken this road and why he was going so fast as he approached the sheer vertical drop to the rocks far below. It would have been so easy to keep going, to put everything behind him, to no longer feel pain.

Pine trees blurred past as the pickup roared down the dirt road to the nothingness ahead. All he could see were sky and more mountains off in the distance. Welcome back to Montana. He'd thought coming home would help. He'd thought he could forget everything and go back to being the man he'd been.

His heart thundered as he saw the end of the road coming up quickly. Too quickly. It was now or never.

The words sounded in his ears, his own when he was young. He saw himself standing in the barn loft looking out at the long drop to the pile of hay below. Jump or not jump. It was now or never.

He was within yards of the cliff when his cell phone rang. He slammed on his brakes. An impulsive reaction to the ringing in his pocket? Or an instinctive desire to go on living?

The pickup slid to a dust-boiling stop, his front tires just inches from the end of the road. Heart in his throat, he looked out at the plunging drop in front of him.

His heart pounded harder. Just a few more moments—a few more inches—and he wouldn't have been able to stop in time.

His phone rang again. A sign? Or just a coincidence? He put the pickup in Reverse a little too hard and hit the gas pedal. The front tires were so close to the edge that for a moment he thought the tires wouldn't have purchase. Fishtailing backward, the truck spun away from the precipice.

Ford shifted into Park and, hands shaking, pulled out his still-ringing phone. As he did, he had a stray thought. How rare it used to be to get cell phone coverage here in the Gallatin Canyon, of all places. Only a few years ago the call wouldn't have gone through.

Without checking to see who was calling, he answered it, his hand shaking as he did. He'd come so close to going over the cliff. Until the call had saved him.

"Hello?" He could hear noises in the background. *"Hello?"* He let out a bitter chuckle. A robocall had saved him at the last moment? he thought.

But his laughter died as he heard a bloodcurdling scream coming from his phone. "Hello?" he yelled. "Who is this?" The scream was followed by a woman's desperate pleas.

"No, please, don't hurt me anymore." Another scream and the sound of breaking glass.

"Hello?" He was yelling, frantic, having no idea who was on the other end of the call—just that she was in trouble. Had the woman meant to call 9ll? Maybe it was

a pocket dial and she hadn't meant to call anyone—let alone a stranger.

"Tell me where you are!" he yelled into the phone, but his voice was drowned out by another scream, this one filled with pure terror—and pain. He knew both too well.

The sound of something hard hitting soft flesh was followed by a choking sound. Choking on blood? The woman was being attacked. By an intruder? Or someone she knew? He'd never felt more helpless as he listened to more breaking glass and the woman's screams.

"No! Please, Humphrey, you're going to kill me! Please. Stay back. Don't make me..." The gunshot sounded deafening—even on the phone. Then there was no sound at all coming from his cell.

Ford stared down at the phone in his hand, shock shuddering through him. The woman on the other end of the line had called the man *Humphrey*. His already pounding heart thumped against his ribs, making his chest ache. It couldn't be. He stared at the name that had come up on his phone. No. He tried to call the number back. It went straight to voice mail. Someone must have found the phone and shut it off. Or declined the call.

His heart was pounding. For a moment, he was too stunned to move, almost to breathe, at what he'd just heard, what he'd been unable to stop. Rachel. The call was from his former college roommate's wife, Rachel Westlake—now Mrs. Humphrey Collinwood.

He'd only recently added her number to his contact list after she'd sent him a friend request on social media and they'd exchanged cell phone numbers.

His pulse pounded so loud that he couldn't hear himself think. Fumbling in his fear and panic, he hit 911.

It couldn't be true. He knew Humphrey. They'd been roommates most of their time in college. His former friend wouldn't hurt anyone. Humphrey idolized Rachel. But from what he'd heard on the call…

Outside the pickup, the wind howled in the pines. A gust blew dirt over the cliff and into the abyss, reminding him how close he'd come to making that same descent. The only thing that had stopped him was the phone call. Or would he have hit the brakes on his own? He would never know.

The 911 operator came on the line. "What is the nature of your emergency?"

"I think I just heard someone being attacked and possibly killed on what I suspect was a pocket dial." His voice broke. "Her name is Rachel Westlake. Sorry, it's Collinwood now." He listened as the dispatcher asked him a question. "No, I don't know where she lives exactly. A ranch north of Big Timber. That's all I know. We only recently reconnected. That's how she had my number. Please, you have to find her. She might still be…alive."

Chapter Two

Dana Cardwell Savage looked out her kitchen window at the row of black clouds gathering over the mountains. She'd awakened this morning with one of her "bad" feelings. Her husband, Hud, used to joke about them. He still didn't necessarily believe in her foreboding "sixth sense." But over their many years together, he'd learned to acknowledge her premonitions with caution, if not take them seriously. Unfortunately, she never knew what was coming—just that something was.

At the sound of a vehicle pulling up in front of the main house on Cardwell Ranch, she squinted into the morning sun to see her cousin Jackson climb out. From the worry etched in his handsome face, she knew even before she opened her front door—someone was in trouble. She ushered him into the kitchen, a place where everyone knew they could get a mug of hot coffee and a kind word—if not advice. Good listener that she was, Dana dispensed it all—and usually with some warm homemade cookies fresh from the oven.

Jackson brushed a lock of hair back from his forehead as he took a seat at her kitchen table. It was large and marred like the floor under it from years of cowboys pulling up a chair and resting their boots under it and their arms on it.

She noticed her cousin's salt-and-pepper hair and felt a shock at how much they had all aged. She didn't feel her age most days. It was only when she looked in the mirror or thought about everything that had happened over the years, the good and the bad.

As she poured her cousin a mug of coffee, she could tell that something was bothering him. She hadn't seen him for a while, but knew that her cousin's barbecue restaurant with his brothers was doing well, so that wasn't the problem.

"Ford's back," Jackson said as he took the mug from her.

Dana brightened as she joined him at the table. She remembered the first time she'd seen the boy when he was about five and Jackson had brought him to the ranch. Such a sweet child. She said as much to his father.

"We'll have to have a party," she said, a part of her brain already making plans. She did love getting all the family together here on the ranch. When Jackson didn't respond, she looked at him closer.

He was holding the mug in his large hands, staring down at the steaming brew in a way that made her heart drop. "What's wrong?"

"Ford's not the same," Jackson said after a moment. "The war, losing his men in the plane crash…" He looked up and she saw fear in his eyes. "I'm worried about him."

She'd heard that Ford had gotten a Purple Heart for his bravery and that he'd saved most of his crew when his plane had crashed. "He wasn't injured, I heard."

"Not physically. But a lot of his crew died. He can't seem to get past it. Why did he survive and not so many others? It's his mental attitude that worries me. He seems…lost. He has a degree in engineering, but doesn't seem interested in pursuing anything. I told him we can find a place for him in the barbecue business…"

"You know he's welcome here on the ranch," Dana said quickly. "In fact, we could really use him. Please tell him that."

Jackson nodded. "As much as he loves the ranch and working here in the past, I doubt even that would help right now."

"Is it PTSD?" she asked.

He shrugged. "Probably. He's been getting help. I just think being over there in that war took the life out of him. He saw too much death, too much pain, just too much." His voice broke and he took a sip of coffee. "I just got a call from him. He's on his way to Big Timber. Seems this woman he knew in college…" He looked up at her. "I shouldn't bother you with this."

"You know I'm here in any way I can help. Ford's family. Why are you worried about this woman?"

"Ford was in love with her. She married his best friend. It wasn't anything he told me, but I have a feeling that this woman did a number on him years ago," Jackson said. "Her coming back into his life right now…"

"She called him for help?"

Her cousin scoffed. "It's much worse than that. She was in a domestic dispute with her husband apparently. For all Ford knows, she might even be dead."

AFTER CALLING 911 and relating what he'd heard, Ford had called his father. He'd given him the abbreviated version of what had happened as he'd driven out of the mountains. He left out the dumbass thing he'd almost done. Just hearing his father's voice was a reminder of the pain he would have caused if he hadn't stopped. He felt embarrassed and guilty.

"I'm on my way to Big Timber now. All I know is that she lives north of town on a ranch. I'll call you when I know something more."

Now he concentrated on the highway in front of him. He was down the east side of the Bozeman Pass when he got a call from the Sweet Grass County sheriff, Charley Cortland.

"You the one who placed the 911 call?" the sheriff asked. His voice was gruff and he sounded like an older man.

Ford explained what had happened—and what he'd heard. "Did you find her? Is she…?" He couldn't bring himself to ask what had happened, fearing she may be dead.

"She's alive. Your call got us to her in time." The sheriff said he'd gone out to her ranch himself and gotten her to the hospital.

He breathed a sigh of relief. On the drive he'd kept remembering a young Rachel in a yellow sundress, her head tilted back, laughing at him and Humphrey. She'd been so beautiful. In his memory, she and Humphrey had looked so happy and so much in love. So what had happened over the past fifteen years to change that?

"How do you know Mrs. Collinwood?" the sheriff asked, pulling him out of his thoughts.

"We were friends back in college. Her husband was

my roommate all four years. I was best man at their wedding."

"I see," the sheriff said. "You said you're on your way here? I'm going to need a statement from you. I'm at the scene, but will be returning to my office soon. One question. Why did she call you instead of 911?"

Ford explained what he suspected had been a pocket dial and how he'd only recently gotten her number and vice versa. "Can you tell me if Humphrey…? Is he…?"

"I'm afraid that's all the information I can give you now. We'll talk at my office. How soon did you say you would be arriving in town?" the sheriff asked.

Ford explained that he was driving from Big Sky, but was now only about an hour away, then disconnected.

Rachel was alive. But how badly injured? As far as he knew, there was only one hospital in Big Timber. Unless she'd been flown to Billings. But that would mean that her injuries were too critical to be taken care of at the local hospital. He knew he had to see for himself that she was all right—and that what he'd heard on the phone had really happened. It felt surreal. He knew Humphrey. They'd been like brothers. And Rachel… He shook his head, not wanting to admit even now the crush he'd had on his best friend's girl.

He passed Livingston, the Crazy Mountains growing closer and closer as he drove. With the speed limit being eighty, he was making good time. The thought of seeing Rachel had him both anxious and excited. He'd hated the way they'd left things for the past fifteen years.

The truth was, he'd never expected to hear from her again after her wedding to Humphrey. After what had happened, the three of them had gone their separate ways. Humphrey had reached out a few times, but Ford hadn't responded. Now he felt sick about that. If Humphrey was gone, he'd never get to make amends.

Then there was Rachel, the woman he'd compared other women to for all these years. Strange how fate worked, he thought now as a chill moved through him. If Rachel hadn't pocket dialed him when she did...she might not have gotten help in time. And Ford...well, he might be at the bottom of a cliff right now.

Chapter Three

"I know who you are," the sheriff said after the medical examiner introduced herself at the crime scene. He hoisted up his tan uniform pants over his protruding belly and rocked back on his boot heels. "I've heard stories about you. You go by Hitch, right? Well, we don't really need your help. George here can handle it just fine."

State medical examiner Henrietta "Hitch" Roberts smiled at the sheriff and the elderly man standing next to him in the entryway of the Collinwood home. "I'm sorry, Sheriff, but the governor himself asked me to handle this one personally. I believe if you check your emails, you'll find one from him."

"Is that so?" Sheriff Charley Cortland tucked his thumbs into the pockets of his pants and narrowed his blue gaze at her. A large fiftysomething man with a robust laugh and a belly to match, Charley had been the law for years. He liked to say to anyone who would listen that he'd seen it all. "George here is our local coroner and I've already assessed the situation. The wife was getting the hell beaten out of her. She grabbed a gun and shot her husband before he could kill her. It's cut-and-dried self-defense, the way I see it. Shot him right in the face."

"Does seem that way at a glance," Hitch said. She'd dealt with her share of rural law enforcement and already heard about Charley Cortland. As state medical examiner, she was brought into those areas that lacked access to more than a local coroner. On this one, she was lead investigator. "My job is to try to find out what really happened here, if at all possible."

She'd already called the Department of Criminal Investigation. By now they would have arrived at the Big Timber hospital and taken photos of the wife's injuries. They would have also collected the clothing she'd been wearing, checked under her fingernails and run gunpowder residue tests on her hands and wrists, as well as getting blood samples to see if she had been under the influence of alcohol or drugs at the time of the shooting—as Hitch had requested. They would have also gotten a video statement from her—if she was able—of what led up to the altercation and subsequent death of the husband.

"We already know what *really* happened," the sheriff snapped. "Got proof. She called someone during the fight and he heard the whole thing. I just got off the phone with him. He's on his way to give me a statement that will back up what I just told you." She listened to the sheriff describe what the caller had related to him. "So she definitely thought he was going to kill her if she hadn't shot him." He had a so-there smug look on his ruddy face.

She pulled out her notebook. "What is the name of the man she called?"

"Ford Cardwell. She married his best friend. He was in the wedding party."

Hitch looked up at him. "He told you that?"

"He did."

"I'll need to talk to him, as well as see the video statement you take from him," she said, pocketing her notebook and pen. "Also, did you document what you saw at the scene on your arrival?"

"I called an ambulance and got the poor woman to the hospital, if that's what you're asking," the sheriff snapped.

"No, I'm asking if you documented the scene." Law enforcement was trained to document everything, including the time of arrival, the location and condition of the body, and determining the identity of the person involved. "Did you observe any vehicles leaving the area?"

The sheriff looked put out. "No. There was just the two of them. Look here, young lady. You're trying to make more out of this than what it is."

"I'm trying to get to the truth," she corrected him. "And you can call me Hitch. Did you observe anything at the scene that seemed out of place?"

He laughed. "Practically anything breakable in the kitchen, I'd say." The coroner he called George laughed with him. "If you just look in the kitchen, you can *observe* for yourself that they had one hell of a fight, with her pleading for him not to kill her."

Hitch could see that she wasn't getting anywhere with the sheriff. He hadn't documented anything and had, in his mind, already solved the case. She glanced past the large living area to the kitchen. Even from here, she could see all the broken pottery and glass on the floor, along with blood and other matter from the body still lying in the middle of it.

"Someone was angry and took it out on the decor, that's for sure," she said. She'd seen this kind of fury before. It often ended in bloodshed.

"Looks like the damned fool had it coming to him," Charley said. "The wife's in the hospital. Beat the hell out of her." He shook his head. "Got to wonder what the two had to fight about, though. Look at this place. Can't even imagine living on a spread this large, let alone in a house like this."

"Guess it proves money can't buy happiness," Hitch said distractedly as she noticed where the sheriff and the coroner had walked through her crime scene. "DCI should be here soon to process the scene. We'll know more after that."

"Seems pretty obvious what happened here," the sheriff was saying. "Self-defense, plain and simple. Can't see why the state crime department had to get involved." He motioned to the body in the other room. "No judge would put her in prison for killing the bastard after what he did to her."

It certainly appeared to be a case of self-defense, but she preferred to wait until all the evidence was in. She said as much to the sheriff again. "So if you don't mind letting me do my job, Sheriff, I'd appreciate it if you would secure the crime scene and make sure no one else tromps through."

The sheriff said something under his breath that Hitch was glad she couldn't hear.

"Why don't we step outside, George, and leave the lady to her…work," the sheriff said.

"It's Hitch. Or Dr. Roberts. And, George, I won't

need your coroner van to transport the body to the morgue. The DCI unit will take care of that for me," Hitch said.

Both men nodded sourly and left. She closed the door behind them and took in the scene before reaching into her satchel for her booties and gloves.

The victim lay on his back on the kitchen floor among broken glass and debris that had apparently originated from the couple's quarrel. The only heads-up she'd been given on the case was an urgent appeal for her to get to the Collinwood Ranch north of Big Timber as soon as possible and take charge of the case. Apparently, there'd been some concern of the crime scene being contaminated.

Fortunately, she'd just finished a case not far away. Otherwise, she was sure George, the local coroner, would have already removed the body. He and the sheriff had already walked into the kitchen. One of them had left a boot print in the blood and then used a paper towel to wipe off the sole.

Along with the urgency of the matter, she'd been told that she would be dealing with what was believed to have been a domestic dispute that had ended in gunplay—and that the wife had been taken to the local hospital with multiple injuries. She hadn't needed to be told that this was a sensitive case because of who was involved. None of that mattered to her. She treated all cases the same.

But she also knew that because the name Collinwood meant something to someone in power, this one would be under the media microscope, so she'd better make sure she left no stone unturned.

Carefully approaching the body through the broken glass, she could definitely tell there had been a violent argument. As she squatted next to the deceased, she could see that he had been shot in the face at close range. The single bullet had entered a half inch off center of his left eye and exited the back of the skull, taking a lot of brain matter and bone with it.

The husband had been so close… Had he been trying to take the gun away from her? Daring her to pull the trigger? Had he been that sure she wouldn't shoot?

Hitch rose to take her camera from the bag slung over her shoulder. She wanted to shoot photographs of the scene before even the state lab unit arrived. As she did, she considered the mess in the large, normally white kitchen. It was a cook's delight with its latest stainless-steel appliances, copper ranch house sink and white marble countertops. The tile floor was also white like the cabinets. It would make the crime scene investigators' jobs even easier, she thought. The perfect crime scene from a forensics standpoint.

At the sound of another vehicle, she looked out to see two DCI vans pull up. The sheriff and coroner had apparently managed to stretch some crime scene tape across the railing on the front deck and outside the door. The sheriff now leaned against his patrol SUV, watching the DCI team emerge from their rigs before he climbed behind the wheel and took off in a hail of dust and gravel.

SHERIFF CHARLEY CORTLAND swore as he roared out of the Collinwoods' ranch, the coroner eating his dust behind him. How dare that young woman treat him as if he didn't know how to do his job. He rubbed his neck with a free hand as he took a turn in the road. He was going too fast, but Hitch, or whatever she wanted to call herself, had gotten his temper up. Coming in like she had and finding fault right away with the way he did things.

Had he documented everything? she'd wanted to know. He thought about the notebook and pen he kept in his patrol SUV. He was sure they were still in his glove box. Glancing in that direction, he almost missed the next turn and finally forced himself to slow down.

What he hadn't realized, but was becoming abundantly clear now that he thought about it, was that this was going to be a big case. The kind of case that could make or break a career. He should have realized that. Hell, he knew the Collinwoods had money once he'd seen the spread—let alone that humongous house they'd had built for themselves.

But lots of rich people bought up the ranches in the area. What made these two so special that the governor would call in the state medical examiner and the DCI?

As he reached the main highway, he stopped and dug out his notebook and pen. From this point on, he would do this one by the book. He could remember well enough the scene when he had arrived, right? He'd put it all down.

The one thing he wouldn't do was let that woman make him look bad again.

Turning on his lights and siren, he raced back toward Big Timber. Just outside town, he called his office. "There a fella waiting to see me?" he barked into his phone. "Tell him I'm on my way."

He disconnected, smiling and nodding to himself. Ford Cardwell had heard the whole thing on his phone and was now cooling his heels in the office. Charley would get his story. If that didn't prove what he was saying about this case, then nothing would. All his years of experience had to account for something, he told himself. Even as he thought it, he found himself questioning his assessment of what had happened with this case.

It was a slam dunk, wasn't it? He couldn't be wrong about this one.

FORD HAD NO trouble finding the sheriff's department when he'd reached Big Timber. He'd been told to take a seat. Ten minutes later, the sheriff arrived in a flurry of movement. A large, heavyset man with a flushed face, the sheriff waved him back into his office. The room was small, unlike the rotund older man who took a chair behind the desk. He had a head of graying hair beneath his Stetson, which he removed and tossed in the direction of a hook on the wall as Ford entered the office.

"Sheriff Charley Cortland," the man said as he shifted his weight, making the chair groan under his considerable bulk. "You say you're Ford Cardwell, right? Let's get your statement while it's still fresh in your mind." He reached for his phone and called in a young man who set up a video recorder, turned it on and left.

"State your name, the time and the date for the record," the sheriff said, and Ford did.

Charley rocked in his chair and nodded. "So you heard the whole thing," he said, urging him on.

"I wouldn't say that. It actually felt as if I had come in toward the end. I heard what I believe was the last of the argument. At first, it was just background noise and then a scream."

"Can you describe from the start of the call everything you heard?"

He took a moment, reliving it, knowing now how it would end. He went through it, finishing with, "At the time, I thought the call had just been random. I didn't know the woman was Rachel Westlake—I mean, Collinwood."

"Right. You knew her in college. So when was the last time you saw her?"

"It's been years—fifteen, actually. Like I told you on the phone, I only recently reconnected with her on social media and we exchanged phone numbers. I haven't seen her since college."

The sheriff nodded, studying him. "But you knew her husband?"

He caught the past tense. "Humphrey? Yes, we all knew each other at college. Wait—so he is…?"

"Deceased."

He had heard the booming report of the gunshot on his phone. "Humphrey's dead?" He felt an anxiety attack coming on and had to concentrate on his breathing for a few moments. His plane crash came back, filling his mind with horror just as it had when he'd realized they were going down and there was nothing he could do about it. Just as there was nothing he could do but save the few men he'd been able to drag from the wreckage before it exploded.

The sheriff's voice brought him out of the flashback with a shudder.

"He was killed this morning during the phone call

you overheard. In fact, I believe you heard the shot that killed him."

Ford closed his eyes for a moment. Flashes of light radiated behind his lids. He opened them, chasing away the flames to face a different kind of horror. Rachel had shot and killed Humphrey.

"You said that he was your best friend."

"In college." He couldn't make sense of this. Humphrey and Rachel? This couldn't be happening. "Humphrey and I were roommates all four years. Look, if that's all, I'm anxious to find out how Rachel is doing." She must be devastated, he thought, not to even mention her physical injuries.

"Cardwell. Why does that name sound familiar?"

"My family owns a barbecue restaurant in Big Sky. My aunt owns a ranch there. Cardwell Ranch." When the sheriff's expression hadn't changed, he added, "Her husband is Marshal Hud Savage." Why was this man avoiding telling him Rachel's condition? "Sheriff, is Rachel all right?"

"I'm waiting to hear from the doctor, but she sustained multiple injuries from the beating she got." The sheriff picked up his phone and called to tell the young man who'd set up the video that they were finished. He said nothing until the man exited with the equipment. "Appears there were only the two of them home. We'll know more once she can tell us her side of the story. But at this point, it seems clear that it was a domestic dispute that turned tragic."

Ford's head reeled. He kept thinking of the call. Of Rachel's screams. Her pleas for Humphrey to stop. And the gunshot just before the line went dead. That had to be when she pulled the trigger and killed Humphrey. *Oh my God, Rachel, how did this happen?*

Chapter Four

Hitch did what investigating she could on the prem-ises until she had the body on the examining table for the autopsy. She'd worked with this team of investi-gators before, so while they processed the scene, she did an inventory of the house. Putting on fresh gloves, she wandered around in fresh paper booties, trying to get a feel for the people who had lived here while she waited for the team to release the body.

All on one level, the house seemed to go on forever. She peeked in each room, not sure what she was look-ing for. Answers, always. Like the sheriff had said, this one seemed cut-and-dried. Mitigated homicide. So what was bothering her? She couldn't put her finger on it. Just that something always nagged at her when a case felt...wrong.

She found the master suite and stopped in the door-way to take in the breathtaking view before entering. A wall of windows looked out on rolling hills lush with grass and studded with pines. She tried to imagine the couple waking up to this each morning. Stepping to the bed, she checked the side tables, curious if the two were still sleeping together before everything went south.

There was a book lying facedown on one side of

the bed. From the title, she guessed Rachel slept on the right. She pulled open the drawer. It seemed a little too empty, as if someone had gone through it, knowing that detectives would be doing the same thing soon.

Stepping to the other side of the bed, she found a notebook and pen. From the writing and what was written there, she guessed it was the husband's notes about a work appointment. She photographed the notes. There was much more in his drawers, though nothing that sent up any red flags. Except for the extra clip of cartridges for a .38 pistol. She photographed everything in both drawers, then hesitated.

If Humphrey Collinwood kept the gun in this drawer, how did it end up in the kitchen, where he died? Which one of them took the gun to the murder scene?

She thought of the .38-caliber weapon lying on the floor of the kitchen earlier. By now, the lab techs would have bagged and processed it. The question was, when did the wife take hold of the gun? Was it always loaded? Had she ever fired it before?

There were always more questions than answers at this point, Hitch thought. When the woman had gotten the gun could indicate premeditation, so it was important—and probably hard to prove since only one person knew the truth. The other one was dead.

So, she thought, studying the king-size bed, it appeared they had been sleeping together. But that didn't mean that things had been copacetic. The bed was huge. They wouldn't even have to touch each other if they didn't want to.

She checked out the his-and-hers walk-in closets, as well as looking in the chests of drawers. She found a lot of expensive clothing on both sides. She took more photographs, not sure which ones might prove important.

It was the small, seemingly trivial things that solved a case, she thought as she checked out the bathroom. She saw expensive beauty products and what appeared to be a container of birth control pills, most of the pills already taken, lying on the floor in the back corner, almost out of sight as if dropped there. Or thrown there? That was interesting. At least one of them wasn't interested in having a child.

As she started to leave the bedroom, she realized what she hadn't seen. The woman's purse. She checked the walk-in again. Lots of empty purses, but not one the woman had apparently been using. Nor had she seen one in the living room or the kitchen. As she wandered through the house, she kept looking. At the entry into the kitchen, she called to the techs.

"Have either of you seen her purse?" Hitch was curious if it was large enough to hold a handgun. Also, if it wasn't here, then where was it? The sheriff was so sure that no one else had been here. Would a ranch this size have some kind of hired help?

"Not in here," one of them called back.

She turned and headed down past the bedrooms again toward the garage. Living this far from civilization, maybe she'd left her purse in her vehicle. Just as Hitch had expected, none of the vehicles were locked. She opened the first one, a Range Rover that smelled of leather and men's aftershave. This would have been his car.

After searching it and not finding much of interest other than a few receipts, which she took photos of with her phone, she tried the next vehicle. It was a

BMW convertible and smelled of the same perfume scent she'd picked up in the master bedroom. No purse, though. No receipts either.

The purse wasn't in the large SUV or the older-model pickup.

"You can have the body now," one of the techs called.

On her way back through the house, she had a thought and checked the powder room by the door to the garage. The moment she opened the door, she pulled up her camera and took a few shots of the room—and the large designer purse lying on the floor in front of the sink. The purse was made of soft leather and had more than enough room for the .38 now lying next to the body in the kitchen.

What had caught her eye was where it lay—on the floor as if it had been dropped there. Also, the large zippered compartment was open, the woman's wallet partially hanging out, as if Rachel Collinwood had been in a hurry and that was why it was open and lying on the floor like that.

Hitch stared at the purse, imagining the woman coming home from town. It was a fairly long drive. Had she come in, headed straight for the powder room and then heard a garage door open, signaling that she was no longer alone? She would have known it was her husband. Had she dug in the bag for the gun? And for her phone, or both, since both were found in the kitchen on the floor next to the body? She'd apparently picked up the phone after shooting her husband and called 911 for help. Hitch had already photographed the phone, covered with bloody fingerprints, lying next to the body.

Then hearing him enter the house, had she dropped

the bag and followed him into the kitchen with the gun and phone? Or hurried into the kitchen to wait for him?

After picking up the purse, Hitch spread out a clean towel and dumped the contents onto the counter by the sink. A small box of handgun cartridges tumbled out. She inspected them. They were .38-caliber cartridges, the same caliber as those used in the handgun that had been on the kitchen floor not far from the body—and was assumed to be the murder weapon.

She put everything back into the purse and returned it to the spot where she'd found it, before going into the kitchen and telling the techs what she'd found. "Definitely want prints on that birth control container," she said.

The investigators put the deceased into a body bag and loaded it into a van. One of them would follow her into town to the morgue and return to finish processing the scene.

"You know who he is, right?" Bradley Mar asked her. She'd worked with the young investigator before on other cases. He was smart, cute and definitely not her type, with his crooked grin and his bedroom brown eyes.

"Humphrey Collinwood," she said. "Is that name supposed to mean something to me?"

"The family is from back East. Old money. The father and grandfather are still powerful politically, and Humphrey was the heir apparent. There was talk that he might one day be president. This case will probably garner nationwide media coverage. Even if she had probable cause to shoot him, I wouldn't want to be in her shoes right now."

Hitch knew what Bradley was saying. Even if it

was self-defense, the Collinwoods could probably want their pound of flesh. She was sure DCI had been warned to be especially careful with the evidence in this case. Any mistakes could cost them all their jobs. The DCI unit was always thorough, but with this one, they would make sure they dotted every *i* and crossed every *t*.

Closing the back of the van, she watched the other investigator return to the house. Lori Stevenson was about the same age as Bradley, but much more serious. Hitch hoped that Lori hadn't already fallen for Bradley's charm. The young man was a heartbreaker. Unfortunately, Hitch knew the type. It was one reason she hardly dated.

Climbing behind the wheel of her SUV, she started the engine and drove away from the huge house set against a backdrop of rolling hills and pasture with mountains off in the distance. As she did, she considered how isolated it was. The drive out was a good two miles to the paved highway. From there, it was another twenty miles into Big Timber. That kind of isolation could get to a person, she thought. Anything could have caused the altercation and subsequent shooting.

In her experience, money was usually the big issue in most marriages. After that it was infidelity. She thought about the rambling house, the two separate walk-in closets filled with expensive clothes and jewelry, the four-car garage with luxury vehicles, the ranch itself with its beautiful vistas.

For most people, this would be paradise, and yet one of the residents was dead and the other in the hospital facing possible homicide charges. So what had happened?

The purse on the floor in the powder room bothered her. It suggested that Rachel Collinwood had been somewhere and had just come in from the garage. Was the husband already home? Or had he just entered the house from the garage, not knowing she was in the powder room? Had the wife known her husband would come home angry? Had she felt she was in danger?

But if the gun had been in her purse along with the .38 cartridges, when had she taken it from her husband's bedside table? And why would she take the gun and her cell phone and go into the kitchen if she was afraid for her life? Why not get back in her car and get out of there?

The sheriff had said the man she'd accidentally dialed had heard it all—including the gunshot before the phone call ended. So had Rachel Collinwood attempted to call 911 for help in the middle of the altercation and accidentally dialed Ford Cardwell instead?

Hitch was anxious to talk to both Mrs. Collinwood and the man she'd called. Her cases often intrigued her, but none more than this one. She tried to put herself in the woman's shoes in that powder room, knowing it was all speculation at this point. But the wife had been in the powder room. The purse proved it. After returning from town? So where was the husband? Just driving in? Or waiting for her in the kitchen?

What had been her state of mind? Panic? Or cold-blooded calm? The purse could have been dropped in terror at the sound of the garage door opening. Rachel could have been in a hurry to reach the kitchen before her husband. Had the husband been looking for her as he moved through the house? Had the argument started somewhere else? Where had they been before the argument? A larger question was also more than relevant.

Had there been prior abuse? Was that why she had the gun? Assuming it had been in the purse and not hidden somewhere else in the house.

All simple conjecture until she had more evidence. The real question for Hitch was, what had been going through the woman's mind when she'd taken the gun from her husband's bedside drawer in the first place— if she had? If Rachel Collinwood had been terrified of her husband, why hadn't she simply gone to the garage, gotten in her car and driven to safety?

In her mind's eye, Hitch could see her standing in the kitchen amid all the debris from the fight. What had she done with the gun? If she'd had it from the start of the argument, she hadn't used it. Had she threatened her husband with it? Or had she come in, dropped the purse in the powder room and hurried into the kitchen to hide the gun, hoping she wouldn't have to use it, until she'd felt she had no choice?

The moment the wife had armed herself, she had made up her mind that she was going to pull that trigger— whether she realized it or not.

AT THE HOSPITAL, Ford waited until the doctor received permission from the sheriff for him to see Rachel. He'd been warned that it would only be for a few minutes.

"She's going to be groggy," the doctor said. "Also, the sheriff has asked that she not be questioned about what happened."

Ford thanked him and headed down the hall to where a uniformed guard sat outside her door. Seeing the man sitting there gave him a shock. At first, he'd thought it was for Rachel's protection. But from whom?

Then he realized with a start—the guard was there to keep Rachel here. Had she been arrested?

He felt sick to his stomach at the thought. But she'd killed a man. And not just any man. A man they had both loved. He couldn't imagine being pushed that far, and yet he'd heard enough of the fight on the phone to be terrified for her. That was why he had to see her and make sure she was all right. While he wouldn't ask anything about the incident as the sheriff had ordered him, he desperately needed to know at some point what had happened that the marriage had ended like this.

As he stopped at her hospital room door, he kept replaying what he'd heard on the phone over and over in his head. He still couldn't believe any of this was real. The scenes in his head kept overlapping with his own tragedy, blurring the lines.

He'd thought he'd known Humphrey. He never would have expected this of him. And Rachel… How long had the abuse been going on that she had to stop her husband with a bullet?

The guard at the door double-checked with the sheriff and then gave Ford a nod. Pushing open the hospital room door, Ford hesitated, not sure he was ready to see the beautiful woman he'd known and loved in whatever state Humphrey had left her.

After taking a breath, he let it out and stepped in. She lay in the bed, her eyes closed, her face as pale as the pillowcase beneath her head—except for the lacerations, stitches, bandages and bruising that made the woman he'd known almost indistinguishable. The extent of her injuries shocked him. He'd just assumed that the quarrel hadn't been going on long when he'd first gotten the call. But Humphrey couldn't have done this much damage in that short amount of time before the gunshot.

All Ford could figure was that at some point, Rachel had tried to call for help and either dropped the phone after accidentally hitting his number or Humphrey had knocked the phone from her hand.

The violence he saw mirrored in her injuries made his chest ache. He felt perspiration break out over his body. He grabbed the metal rail of the bed to steady himself as he felt another anxiety attack coming on.

THE RATTLE OF the bed rail awoke her with a start. Rachel let out a cry. She'd forgotten for a moment where she was. She shrank back from the dark figure beside her bed.

"I'm sorry. I didn't mean to frighten you," Ford said as he quickly took a step back.

She recognized his voice. It was low and soft and soothing, always had been. As her gaze focused on him, she tried to smile, but her cut and bruised mouth hurt too much. "Ford." His name came out a whisper. She felt tears rush to her eyes at just the sight of a friendly, familiar face in the middle of all her pain.

As she held out her hand, he moved closer and took it in his two large, warm palms. It had been years since she'd seen him, so she shouldn't have been shocked that he'd changed. His body had filled out from the lean college boy he'd been. If anything, he was more handsome. She'd heard what had happened to him during his time in the military and wondered how an experience like that would change a man like Ford. She could see now that there was a hardness to him that was only partially due to muscle and physical strength. There was also a darkness in his pale blue eyes.

"*Ford?* I'm so glad to see you, but what are you doing here?"

"I heard what happened to you," he said. "Are you all right?"

She shook her head, tears rushing to her eyes again. "Humphrey." The word came out choked on fresh tears.

He nodded and squeezed her hand. As he looked down at her fingers entwined with his, she thought about earlier when two state crime investigation officers had stopped by to take her fingerprints and take swabs of her skin around her hands and wrists. When she'd asked, they'd told her they were checking for gunpowder residue, and that brought it all back. The deafening sound of the gun. The damage the bullet made an instant later.

But more than anything, what she kept seeing was the shocked, disbelieving look on her husband's face. She would take that look to her grave.

Ford squeezed her hand gently. "I'm here for you." She looked at him, knowing he meant every word of it. She'd forgotten this side of Ford and felt her throat tighten.

"I can't believe any of this has happened," she said, wiping at the tears with her free hand as she focused on his face. To think she had actually thought about marrying this cowboy, she told herself, then pushed the thought away as her pain threatened to overwhelm her again.

"What about you? Are *you* all right?" she asked when she gained control again. "I heard about your accident… I'm so sorry."

"Don't worry about me," he said quickly. "I'm fine. It's you I'm concerned about. But I'm here for you. Whatever I can do. I'm not going anywhere."

At the sound of the hospital room door opening, she glanced toward it and saw a man in uniform and star enter. She swallowed the lump in her throat at just the sight of the sheriff's grim expression. Only hours ago she'd been standing in her kitchen with the gun in her hand and her finger on the trigger. She closed her eyes but felt fresh tears on her cheeks as Ford let go of her.

She heard him step away from her bed as the sheriff said, "I need to talk to Mrs. Collinwood. Alone. But don't go far, Mr. Cardwell. I'll need a word with you, as well."

Rachel smelled peppermint on the sheriff's breath as she heard him pull up a chair beside her bed. She heard Ford's boots on the hospital room floor, the slow, deliberate gait of his walk and the swish of the door opening and closing.

"Mrs. Collinwood, you remember me? I'm Sheriff Charley Cortland. I'm the one who called for an ambulance for you. The doctor said you might be a little groggy, but I need you to answer a few questions if you feel up to it."

Rachel opened her eyes, turning her head to look at the man. What she saw made her relax a little. There was kindness in his weathered face rather than accusation. She wiped her eyes and said, "I'll tell you everything I can remember."

The hospital room door opened again. This time a young man came in with a video recorder. He set it up next to her bed. She touched the bandage on her cheekbone and realized she probably shouldn't be thinking about her appearance at a time like this.

"Don't worry—you look fine," the sheriff said. "We just need to get your statement while it's fresh in your mind so everyone knows what happened."

Chapter Five

Hitch looked up as a distinguished older man in a suit burst into the morgue. He had a head of salt-and-pepper hair and keen gray eyes with deep crinkles around them. His skin appeared ashen under his tan, and his hand shook as he clutched the doorknob and looked around the autopsy room.

"Where is the medical examiner? I want to see my son," he demanded.

She'd been expecting Bartholomew Collinwood. "I'm the medical examiner. Henrietta Roberts," she said. "If you give me a few minutes, you are welcome to make an identification for the record."

He stared at her in surprise and then what might have been slight embarrassment. He seemed to check his anger as she asked him to please wait outside the autopsy room. "I'll have someone show you where you can have a seat." She thought he would object. But then he looked past her to where the body bag was being unloaded from the state investigators' van.

The realization made him stagger a little before he caught himself and turned back into the hallway, letting the door close behind him.

She hurried to help roll the body into the morgue.

Once she had it on the examination table, she went to find Mr. Collinwood. He was sitting on a bench outside, his head in his hands.

"If you'd like to come with me now," she said quietly. She never got used to the amount of grief she witnessed. She hoped she never did.

It took him a moment to rise from the bench. He was a man who clearly carried himself with unsparing confidence, and she saw that he was now struggling to maintain it. She often saw this kind of debilitating grief and felt it clear to her core. In these rural areas of the state, she was often alone in these duties of telling friends and family of their loss.

The hardest part was asking them to identify the bodies. Usually, that fell to the local coroner unless she'd been called in on a case.

If the dead man hadn't been Humphrey Collinwood, killed by his wife, Rachel Collinwood, then right now George would be doing this, she thought as she led Bart Collinwood into the morgue to identify his son.

FORD WONDERED WHY the sheriff wanted to see him again, but he stayed around the hospital. Down in the cafeteria, he got himself a cup of coffee. At the smell of the evening meal, he realized he hadn't eaten all day. No wonder he felt weaker than usual. But he suspected he wouldn't be able to get a bite down right now.

Back up on Rachel's floor, he parked himself in the waiting room and sipped his beverage. It was hot and bitter, which suited him just fine. He thought of Humphrey, but quickly pushed his image away. Instead, he tried to remember how it had all started and realized that would have been the moment he first saw Rachel. The moment Humphrey also saw her and Ford lost her.

It had been in the park near the university. He and Humphrey had been sitting on the grass under a large oak tree like they usually did after their chem class when a woman had caught Ford's eye. She was a vision in an orange-and-white polka-dot sundress that accented her slim, sun-kissed form. She was trying to feed a squirrel a scrap of bread from her lunch. He watched her for a few minutes, amused by her patience. Humphrey had been lying back on the grass, smoking and staring up at the blue sky overhead. Ford had been leaning back against a tree, watching the world go by.

He remembered that carefree feeling with his whole life ahead of him. It had felt as if anything was possible. That was when Rachel had caught his eye. She and the squirrel chattering at her from a nearby tree. What fascinated him was the way she could hold so perfectly still, kneeling on the grass, her arm extended, the scrap of bread pinched between two fingers. He'd been impressed by her perseverance, her naive belief that if she waited long enough the squirrel would come to her.

He hadn't been able to help himself. He'd pulled out the cell phone he'd gotten for Christmas and snapped a photo of her. The movement caught not just her eye, but also that of the squirrel, which took off up the tree.

Getting to her feet, she'd mugged a face at him as he'd gotten up and walked over to her. "I'd almost had him convinced to take the bread." It was a rebuke.

Ford had laughed. "That squirrel was never going to take that bread."

"How do you know that?" she'd demanded, glaring at him.

"I heard what he was saying to you." He'd grinned. "He doesn't eat white bread."

Her face had softened into a glorious smile, one that would haunt his dreams for years to come. "You understand squirrels?"

"Clearly better than you," he'd joked. "I'd be happy to teach you, though. I'm Ford Cardwell, squirrel whisperer."

Her smile had broadened as she said, "Rachel Westlake. You do know that has to be the worst pickup line I've ever heard." Her gaze had shifted to Humphrey, who had spotted the two of them and gotten up to join them.

Ford had taken one look at his friend's face and known that he'd been as captivated by the woman as Ford had been. The difference was that Rachel had been looking at Humphrey with that same expression.

Rachel and Humphrey used to joke that it had been love at first sight. Ford knew it had been for him, not that he'd ever told anyone, especially the two of them. Rachel and Humphrey had started dating after that, the three of them often together. He thought of all the photos with Humphrey with one arm around Rachel and one around Ford. Humphrey always said that he couldn't live without either of them. It had been like that right up through graduation and their wedding.

Now in the waiting room, he felt that old guilt and pain. What hurt was how much he'd missed his best friend the past fifteen years and now Humphrey was gone.

As the waiting room door opened, Ford started. He'd expected it to be the sheriff. Instead, it was a man he'd only met a few times but recognized at once.

Bartholomew "Bart" Collinwood walked in as if he owned the hospital. He certainly could have bought it if he wanted to, Ford knew. Humphrey and his father had had a tense relationship back in college. His friend always felt that he would never live up to his father's expectations. Ford wondered if that had changed over the years.

Bart stopped short in the middle of the room and frowned as he stared at him. "Ford, isn't it?"

"Ford Cardwell." He was a little surprised the man even remembered him.

"I recall you saying it was an old Texas family name, right? Or was it Montana?" The shock of his son's death wore heavily on the man. He seemed confused and unsure of himself for a moment. Then his gaze seemed to clear. "You know, you're the reason my son bought the ranch out here. All those stories you used to tell about ranch life."

He heard accusation in the man's tone. Did he believe that if his son hadn't bought a ranch in Montana he'd still be alive? Ford didn't know what to say, so he said nothing. The man was grieving. He was probably also looking for someone to blame.

"You two were good friends, roommates," Bart continued. "Had a falling-out at the end of your senior year at college, right?"

Was that how Humphrey had explained it? "I joined the military," Ford said.

"That's right." The man shook his head. "I'm surprised my son didn't follow you right into boot camp since he wanted to do whatever you did. Rachel knew how much he admired you. She must have stopped him. She wouldn't have allowed him to do anything but make more money for her to spend."

Ford shook his head, recalling that Bart had never been a fan of Rachel's. "Humphrey loved her."

The man let out a bitter laugh that almost sounded like a sob. "And look what it cost him."

Ford started to argue that Humphrey hadn't been the only victim in what had happened, but Bart cut him off.

"So you're here for his wife."

Was that an accusation or just Ford's guilt making him hear it that way? "It isn't like that."

"It sure looks like that."

The sheriff stuck his head into the door of the waiting room, drawing both of their attention. Bart moved swiftly to the lawman and grabbed his arm as he began demanding justice for his son.

The sheriff shook him off. "I thought you might be here wanting to know how his wife is doing after being severely beaten almost to death by your son," Charley Cortland said. "She's recovering nicely."

Bart huffed. "I want to see her."

"I don't think that's a good idea," the sheriff said. "You're just going to upset her and she's been through enough."

"*She's been through enough. She killed my son!* I was just at the morgue. She shot him in the *face*!" Bart's voice broke with emotion. "I *will* see her. She *will* look me in the eye and tell me the truth."

At the raised voices, a security guard pushed open the waiting room door.

The sheriff turned toward the uniformed man. "Hal, show this gentleman out of the hospital. If he comes back, let me know so I can arrest him."

"You have no idea who you are dealing with," Bart said angrily. "You'll be lucky to be the dogcatcher when I get through with you."

Chapter Six

Back at the morgue, dressed and ready for the autopsy, Hitch studied the corpse lying now on the metal table. After Mr. Collinwood had left, she'd gone online. It had been easy to find information about Humphrey Collinwood and his wife, Rachel. He'd been handsome, wealthy and a successful businessman. There were dozens of shots with him and his wife at gala affairs and fund-raisers before they'd moved from New York City to the ranch north of Big Timber, Montana. The two had been photographed at every party they attended as the VIPs they were.

That had been until about a year ago, when they'd bought the ranch and moved here, from what Hitch could tell. Was that the beginning of the end?

She'd also done research on Ford Cardwell. A cowboy turned hero flyboy who'd received a medal of honor after his plane had crashed because of a mechanical failure in war-torn Afghanistan. Miraculously surviving the crash, he'd fought to save his crew, rescuing some but losing others when the plane exploded. He'd only left the military a few months ago. Interesting, she'd thought. Before that, it had appeared he was making the military his career.

But what intrigued her more was how he'd gotten involved in Humphrey Collinwood's death.

Pulling up her mask, she turned on her video recorder and began the autopsy.

Cause of death: a single gunshot wound. She went through the steps, documenting each into the camera.

She frowned as she noticed the deceased's hands. If he had been beating his wife, there would have been bruises, abrasions, some sign of trauma.

Carefully, she removed first his wedding ring and bagged it. Then the ring on his other hand. His right hand. It was large, gold and heavy with a diamond at its center. She noted the blood and skin that had been caught in the design before taking a sample and bagging the ring. If he'd been right-handed, then this was the hand he would have used to hit his wife.

Still, the lack of abrasions or bruising on his hands bothered her. She took photographs of each hand. But until Hitch saw the extent of her injuries, she wouldn't know if he had used something other than his fists.

The sheriff had already decided it had been a case of self-defense. But she knew most were never as simple as that. Had Rachel Collinwood feared for her life? Had she used the proper amount of force based on that fear? Had she shot to stop the man or kill him? Hitch recalled one case where the location of the gun had been a deciding factor in whether or not the woman had planned to kill her husband—and whether she was exonerated.

Rachel had a witness of sorts already waiting in the wings. Hitch couldn't wait to meet Ford Cardwell and hear how it was that his old friend from college just happened to call him at one of the most tragic times of her life.

"HOW LONG ARE you going to be in town?" the sheriff asked Ford after the security guard left with Bart in tow.

"I'm not sure yet," Ford told him. "I'm not leaving right away. I want to be sure that Rachel's all right. Truthfully, I also would like some answers. I still can't believe any of this. Humphrey was like a brother to me. This just doesn't make any sense."

"People change," the sheriff said. "Either that or he was always like that and just hid it well."

After being told that Mrs. Collinwood was down in X-ray and he wouldn't be able to see her again until tomorrow, Ford left. He'd just walked out the front of the hospital when he saw a woman etched against the last of the sunset. She stood off the sidewalk, at the edge of the deep shadows that had settled in around the hospital. It had been a long day, so no wonder he thought he was seeing things. The woman resembled someone he used to know. He was about to turn toward his pickup when the woman spotted him and called his name.

"That is you, isn't it?" she said as she stubbed out her cigarette and moved from the shadows so he got a good look at her.

"Shyla?" He couldn't help his surprise. Like with Rachel, it had been years since he'd seen her best friend from college. He frowned. How had she known about what had happened and gotten here this quickly? "What are you doing here?"

"The same thing you are, I would imagine," she said. "Have you seen Rach? Is she okay? The guard wouldn't let me in to see her."

"I mean, how did you get to Montana so quickly? Did you fly in with Bart?"

"Bart? Good Lord, no! I live here now. I guess you haven't heard. My last name's Birch now. I married a cowboy." She laughed. It was high-pitched and loud—just like it had been in college. Like Humphrey, Shyla had come from old money. It was no surprise that she'd said at college that her family considered her the black sheep. "I know. It was my dream, right?"

"How long have you lived here?" he asked.

"I was out here visiting Rach a year ago and…" She waved a hand through the air. "It just kind of happened. Listen, if you aren't doing anything right now, I could really use a drink. Think we can find a bar close by?"

Ford had to smile. Shyla Earhart hadn't changed in the least. Brash, abrasive, loud and completely without filters. He didn't want or need a drink, but he needed to know about Rachel and what had led up to today's tragedy.

"I'm betting that you already have a bar in mind," he said.

She laughed again and looped her arm through his. "You know me so well. So how have you been, Ford?"

"Just dandy," he lied as they walked to his pickup.

The bar Shyla chose was small and dark and surprisingly quiet. It definitely wasn't a cowboy bar. He wondered idly about her husband and how they'd met, but after getting them two drinks from the bar, he asked about Rachel.

"So what happened with Rachel and Humphrey?" he asked.

Shyla mugged a face. "He turned out to be a real bastard." She quickly raised a hand as if she thought he would argue and rushed on. "I know he was your friend, but he'd changed." She grimaced. "You have no idea how bad it got once they moved out here. Rach didn't want to move here, you know. She hated living out in the sticks. Like he cared. He was often gone to the big city on business, so she was out there, terrified in that big house, all alone. That's why I came out to stay with her for a while and ended up meeting my cowboy and getting married. My family had multiple heart attacks over it." She laughed and picked up her drink.

"Did you know he was abusive to her?" Ford asked as Shyla drained her glass and signaled the bartender for another. He hadn't even touched his yet.

"Sure, I knew. I mean, I'd seen the bruises a couple of times. She always had a story. Walked into a wall. Got hit by a tree branch. Fell off her horse. The usual." Shyla rolled her eyes. "I knew something was wrong."

"Why didn't she leave him?" He took a sip of his drink.

"Why do you think? His father forced her to sign a prenup before they got married. Divorce was out of the question unless she wanted to live like a pauper."

"She could have gotten a job."

Shyla laughed. "Rachel? She majored in psychology at college and hasn't worked all these years. You want fries with that?"

"But if he was abusing her—"

"He traveled a lot and it didn't happen all the time, but I had suspected it was getting worse when he returned to the ranch. When they first married, she'd wanted kids. He didn't. You knew about the miscarriage, right? Then they moved out here and he decides he wants kids. She reminds him that she can't get pregnant. Something about that miscarriage after their wedding. He wants to adopt. At thirty-two, she felt like that ship had sailed."

"A lot of women are having babies later in life," he said.

"Not with a husband who is abusive," Shyla said, leaning toward him. He could smell cigarette smoke and her cloying perfume mixing with the booze she'd drunk. "He was a spoiled rich kid and he wasn't happy, so he took it out on her."

He didn't remember that about Humphrey. Sure, his friend came from wealth, but he'd seemed almost embarrassed by it. Ford reminded himself that he was getting only one side of the story: Rachel's, as told to Shyla. But then again, that might be the only side he was ever going to get now.

"She might go to prison," he said.

Shyla's eyes widened. "How is that possible? For killing the bastard when he was trying to kill her?"

"I heard a lot of it while it was happening," he said. She froze. "You *what*?"

"Rachel called me. I heard her screaming and pleading with him not to hurt her—"

"Wait. You two have been talking?"

"No. She contacted me on social media recently. We exchanged phone numbers. That's all it was. I never planned to call her…"

"She called you for help?"

He shook his head. "It wasn't like that. I think she pocket dialed me by accident. Anyway, I heard all of it right up to the gunshot before the call ended."

"You told the sheriff this?" He nodded. "Then there is no way she's going to prison, Ford. Clearly, it was self-defense, right?"

"It sure sounded that way," he said as he finished his drink and she downed her second one.

Her cell phone rang. He could hear only one side of the conversation but it seemed pretty clear. Her husband was reminding her that she was supposed to be cooking dinner and she needed to get home.

"We should go," he said, although Shyla had told her husband that she'd be home when she was good and ready and it was high time he learned to cook.

She smiled almost sheepishly. "He really is a good guy. Just a little too much sometimes."

He took her back to the hospital where she'd left her car. "Are you going to try to see Rachel again?"

"Tomorrow," Shyla said as he walked her to her car. It had gotten dark while they were in the bar. She opened her car door and turned to look at him. "Is it bad? What he did to her?" Ford nodded. "She was lucky he didn't kill her. You asked what happened between them. She thought he was having an affair. And get this—it was with a local woman who works as a waitress at the Corner Café in town. Emily Sutton."

"You know her?" he asked.

She shook her head. "Rachel only told me a couple of days ago. She'd just found out. I went by the café after that, but Emily wasn't working, and the next thing I knew, I heard about what had happened out at the ranch earlier today. Thanks for the drinks." She climbed into her car and drove away.

Ford watched her go. Shyla was out here in Montana married to a cowboy. He couldn't believe that any more than he could that Humphrey was having an affair, had beaten Rachel and she'd felt forced to kill him. But as the sheriff said, people changed. Ford wondered if the alleged affair was what the two had argued about. Or was it about adopting children?

His cell phone rang. He pulled it out, saw that it was his father and realized he wasn't in the mood to explain everything that had happened today. Or how he found himself involved again in Rachel's life. He knew his father wouldn't have thought it was a good idea. Jackson had met Rachel and Humphrey back in college. And while his father had been taken with Humphrey, he hadn't been a fan of Rachel's. Or maybe what his father hadn't liked was Ford's obvious infatuation with the woman who was clearly more infatuated with Humphrey than his son.

Ford wasn't getting involved with Rachel. But he didn't want to argue the point, so he texted back, saying he was fine and would be away for a few days. Not to worry. Then he went looking for a place to stay.

HITCH WAS JUST finishing up the autopsy when the sheriff stuck his head in the door.

"About done?" he asked, sounding impatient and out of sorts.

She looked at the clock on the wall in surprise. She hadn't realized how late it was. Behind the sheriff, she could see through a far window that it was dark outside. She'd lost track of time—as she often did. But she had needed to get on this one right away.

"I should have the report to you by tomorrow afternoon," she said. "Do you have a minute?"

He had started to leave. She could tell he wanted nothing to do with the autopsy room. After shrugging out of her garb, she washed her hands and stepped out into the hallway with him.

"Tell me it's a slam dunk," he said. "Gunshot to the face, I don't really need to ask the cause of death."

"I was wondering about the woman's injuries. You were the first one on the scene, right?"

"Like I told you, I found her in the kitchen, sitting on the floor, leaning against a cabinet, looking terrified. She was still holding the gun in one hand and the phone in the other. She dropped both when she saw me and tried to get to her feet. The floor was slick with her blood and his. I had to help her up." He grimaced as if recalling the scene. "I could see that she was in bad shape and that he was dead. I could see what happened. What more is there to say?"

"There is no doubt that she fired the fatal kill shot," Hitch said as she pulled out her phone to consult the report DCI had sent her. "The techs found gunpowder residue on her hands and wrists along with the clothing she was wearing at the time." Slacks, blouse, heels. Dressed like a woman spending the day on the ranch? Or one who'd been to town?

"That seems pretty obvious since there was just the two of them in the house," the sheriff said sarcastically. "She fired the gun and killed him. It wasn't like he shot himself in the face."

"Did she say anything to you about what had happened?"

"Like confess? She was hysterical, in pain, bleeding. I handed her my handkerchief."

"The lab will want that if you still have it," she said, making him roll his eyes.

"You're just going to beat this one like a dead horse, aren't you?" He shook his head. "Let the state get involved and they'll blow this up for no good reason…

Fine." He pulled out the soiled handkerchief from his pocket. She could see only a few spots of blood and something dark. Gunpowder residue? As he tried to hand it to her, she made him wait until she grabbed an evidence bag, getting her another eye roll.

"So she didn't say anything about shooting her husband?" Hitch asked again as she sealed the bag.

"No. She just cried. Clearly, she was in a lot of pain." His jaw muscles clenched and unclenched. "I interviewed her at the hospital. Before you ask, I videotaped her statement."

"Thank you, Sheriff. Oh," she said as she started to turn away and pretended to change her mind. "I'll need to see any statements you've taken, including the ones from Ford Cardwell and Rachel Collinwood."

"I'll call my office and tell them to send you both video interviews." He didn't move for a moment and she could tell he was chewing on something. "I'm damned good at my job, I'll have you know. It's why I've been in this office as long as I have." With that, he turned and left.

She felt the weight of the day. Often she worked late rather than eat alone at some restaurant before going back to an empty motel room. If she didn't love her work so much...

Turning out the light, she started to leave when she looked out to see a pickup parked outside. The lights were on and the engine was running, but she couldn't make out who was behind the wheel.

As if the driver had seen her staring out the window, he sped off. Was it a male driver? She'd just assumed so. She watched until the taillights disappeared around a corner, surprised by the anxious feeling she'd gotten. The driver had just been sitting out there as if watching her. She didn't spook easily, but being alone this late here at the morgue and seeing the driver of the pickup just sitting there…

She shook it off, telling herself it had been nothing. Just a long day and the violent case she'd found herself embroiled in. Tomorrow she would be getting a call from the governor wanting answers. She hoped she had some by then.

Chapter Seven

After a rough night filled with nightmares, Ford showered and drove down to the Corner Café Shyla had mentioned for breakfast. He was curious about the kind of woman his old friend would jeopardize his marriage over. If true. His head ached from the images that had played in his mind and kept him from sleep.

He kept seeing Rachel's bruised and battered facc. But it was Humphrey, once his best friend, who haunted his nightmares the worst. In them, the man had been pleading with Ford to forgive him, as if it had been Ford who'd pulled the trigger on that gun.

He took a seat in an empty booth and waited. The café was busy. He saw there were several waitresses scurrying around. One had short dark hair. The other, long blond hair tied back. Humphrey had always preferred blondes. He figured this one had to be Emily Sutton. When the woman came to his table with a menu tucked under her arm, a glass of water and pot of coffee, he got his first good look at her and felt a start.

She could have been a young Rachel with her big blue eyes and bee-stung mouth. "Coffee?" she asked, smiling. He could only nod, still taken aback. She righted the cup in the saucer that was already on the table and poured, commenting on the beautiful summer day outside, then said, "I'm Emily. I'll give you a minute to look over the menu. But don't worry—I'll be back." Her smile was devastating in its beauty and innocence—just as Rachel's had been all those years ago.

Humphrey would have seen the similarities between the waitress and his wife. Would it have been like falling for Rachel all over again?

Ford opened his menu, surprised at the impact the realization had made on him. What had happened between Rachel and Humphrey? Had he just been looking for a newer model? How deep had the rift between them gotten that it had led to such a catastrophic ending?

He tried to concentrate on his menu. He hadn't been hungry for a very long time. Loss of appetite was only one symptom, he'd been told. As if he didn't know the rest of them. He was apparently the poster boy for post-traumatic stress disorder. He had it all, from the flashbacks, memory loss and nightmares, to the severe anxiety, the emotional numbness and feelings of hopelessness—right down to the despondent suicidal thoughts.

He started to close the menu, thinking he should go back to Big Sky. Rachel didn't need him. Anyway, there was nothing he could do to help her. Other than what he'd already done. His cell phone rang. He saw that it was from the hospital and quickly picked up. His heart rate did a little bump as he heard Rachel's voice on the other end of the line.

"Are you all right?" he asked as he hurried to take the call outside.

"I'm much better, thank you. I was hoping you were still around."

"I am."

"I'm so glad to hear that. I need to see you." The café door opened as several people exited. The clatter of dishes and laughter followed them out, along with the smell of bacon. "You're having breakfast. Please, finish eating. They're taking me down to X-ray again, but then I should be back in my room in the next hour. Come see me?"

"I will." To his surprise, when he disconnected he felt like going back inside the café. The smell of food that had nauseated him earlier now made his stomach rumble. He sat down and the waitress hurried right over.

"Have you decided?" Emily asked. On closer inspection, she wasn't as pretty as Rachel.

He nodded and ordered the special, flapjacks and bacon.

"Good choice," she said and hurried off.

Ford picked up his coffee cup and took a sip. Rachel wanted to see him. What was it he'd heard in her voice? Fear and something else, something he remembered from a very long time ago. He heard her words from fifteen years ago at the wedding. "It should have been you, Ford." And then her mouth and hands were on him and he was kissing her—the woman who'd just married his best friend.

That memory had always come with guilt like a weight around his neck. This morning it didn't feel so heavy. Maybe even just hours after the wedding, Rachel had realized the mistake she'd made.

He felt lighter. He'd been wrong. Rachel *did* need

him. He hadn't realized how much he'd needed her right now, he thought. She'd saved his life on the mountain. Not that he would know if he would have gone through with it. But he felt as if she had literally pulled him back from the brink. Maybe he could do the same for her. At least for the moment it would give his life meaning.

BACK FROM X-RAY, Rachel itched to get her bandages off, head home and soak in a hot bathtub. She had a slight concussion. Her ribs were cracked, not broken. Same with her cheekbone. She felt dirty, grimacing when she saw the dried blood still under her fingernails. Emotions, hot and fierce, bubbled to the surface. Was it her blood? Or was it Humphrey's? The thought of his blood made her wince.

She closed her eyes, wishing for sleep. Last night she'd lain awake, haunted by the memory of her husband's face—and what she'd seen in those blue eyes—that instant before she'd pulled the trigger. Where once there had been such love, such admiration, such gratitude, she'd seen— She couldn't bear to think about it or what their lives had come to.

At college, Humphrey had been the shy, wealthy young man who studied hard, partied little and dated even less. She'd expected him to be cocky the first time she met him after finding out who he was. Instead, he'd been sweet. It didn't surprise her that Humphrey and Ford were good friends. They'd been a lot alike. Ford hadn't even seemed to notice how wealthy his friend's family was. But that was Ford. Money had never mattered to him.

Ford. Of course, he'd been there when she'd needed

him. If only she had married him, she thought, then remembered what he'd said when she'd asked him what he planned to do after graduation.

"Maybe work in the barbecue business with the family. Although I think I'd like to work on Cardwell Ranch with my dad's cousin Dana first. I've spent a lot of time there growing up over the years. It holds special memories for me."

Rachel had been shocked at how little he'd wanted. "You must have another dream. Aren't you majoring in engineering?"

He'd actually laughed and said he didn't need to set the world on fire. He just wanted to have a simple life and give his kids what he'd gotten growing up, an appreciation for Montana living and family. "What I've learned would come in handy on the ranch."

"But didn't I hear Humphrey say that he could get you a job with his dad?" she'd said.

Ford had looked shocked. "That was nice of him, but that's not the life I want."

Was that when she'd been glad that she hadn't set her sights so low? Ford was nice, but she needed more. She needed his roommate because she'd dreamed of the nicer things in life.

She cringed at the memory. Humphrey was dead, while it had been Ford who'd come to her rescue. She had a flash of memory of her lovely kitchen covered in shattered glass and pottery, with Humphrey lying in the middle of it. That vision now served as a nightmare snapshot of her shattered dreams. She closed her eyes tightly, trying to wipe it all away.

At the sound of someone coming into her hospital room, she opened her eyes and braced herself. This waking nightmare wasn't over any more than the ones that ruined her sleep. In fact, she feared the horror was just beginning.

FORD HAD STARTED down the hallway toward Rachel's room when a female voice called after him. Turning, he saw an attractive brunette woman wearing jeans, boots and a Western shirt headed toward him.

"Mr. Cardwell?" she asked when she reached him.

The title felt wrong. "I'm Ford Cardwell."

She held out her hand. She had pale green eyes under dark lashes. "Henrietta Roberts, state medical examiner. Most people just call me Hitch. I'd like to ask you a few questions, if you don't mind. The doctor said we could use his office down the hall, if you'll please follow me." She didn't wait for an answer. Everything about her said she had authority, from the steel in her spine, to the tone of her voice and the no-nonsense look in those eyes. He gathered that she was a woman used to giving orders and having them followed.

He hesitated, though, anxious to see Rachel. She should be back from X-ray. She would be waiting for him. "I was just going to see—"

The medical examiner stopped to look back at him, seeming almost amused. "She isn't going anywhere. I promise you. This way."

In the doctor's office, she closed the door behind them and told him to take a seat. To his surprise, she didn't go behind the desk and take the doctor's chair. Instead, she pulled up the second one in front of the physician's desk. Their knees were only a few inches apart.

Taking out her phone and notebook and pen, she said, "I'd like to record this, if it's all right with you."

"You do know that I already did this at the sheriff's office, right?"

"Yes, but if you don't mind, I'd like to hear it directly from you." She set up her phone to record on the edge of the desk so it was facing him. "I understand you know those involved. Can you please explain?"

He did, going over his relationships with Humphrey and Rachel and then the phone call and what he'd heard.

"So you never heard the victim say anything."

"Is that what you're calling him?" Ford asked. "What does that make Rachel?"

"At this point, they're both victims. I'm trying to find out what happened so I can sort this out. So voices. You heard…"

"The only person I heard was Rachel. I thought at the time that she was being attacked by an intruder. I could hear glass breaking and her screaming…"

"Humphrey never spoke before she called him by name?"

"No."

"Did you hear anything else in the background other than breaking glass?"

"Not that I can remember."

"When you knew Rachel in college, do you know if she owned a gun?"

"No. I mean, no, she didn't. She hated guns."

"Did she learn how to shoot one, that you were aware of?"

"I have no idea. I hadn't seen her for fifteen years until yesterday." He remembered telling her goodbye the day he'd left. More memories hit him like typhoon winds, making a rushing sound in his ears.

"It's clear to me that you care a great deal about her."

Was he that transparent? He started to deny it, but decided to save his breath. "I was half in love with her way back when. I was young. We all were young, that is. But like I said, that was years ago."

"Humphrey Collinwood was your roommate and your best friend, you said. Did the friendship survive the years?"

He didn't know how to answer that. He could feel her studying him with those sea green eyes that seemed to notice everything. "We drifted apart."

She nodded. "You said the last time you saw her was at her wedding to Humphrey?"

He realized he must have told the sheriff that and now she was making too much out of this. He nodded, wishing he'd denied having feelings for Rachel.

"Did Humphrey know how you felt about her?" Those eyes widened. "Did you ever consider getting back at him?"

The accusation caught him flat-footed. He glanced at her phone. Was it still recording? "What are you suggesting? Yes, I had a crush on Rachel years ago, but I wasn't…jealous, not like that."

"I find it interesting that it was your phone number that she called during the altercation with her husband."

"I explained that—"

"So just a few weeks ago, she contacts you out of the blue on social media. Whose idea was it to exchange phone numbers?"

He shook his head. "I don't remember." But when he thought about it, he did. It had been Rachel's.

"Also, you drove right here, making really good time apparently, after the call."

"I was worried after what I'd heard. I knew the sheriff would want to talk to me." He couldn't believe what she was insinuating. "Wouldn't you have done the same thing after hearing something like that involving old friends?"

She didn't answer. "You don't find it a little odd she just happened to call *you*?"

"I explained that. It must have been—"

"A pocket dial, right. Making you a defense witness. Was Rachel surprised when you showed up here?" She didn't give him a chance to answer. "I didn't think so. She knew you would come to her rescue after the call since you were old friends. She had to have known how you felt about her. Even though you'd lost touch for fifteen years, she'd known you'd come when called."

Ford didn't like where this was going. "You'd have to ask her. Look, if we're about finished here..." He stood.

The medical examiner turned off the video on her phone. "I'm assuming you're planning to stay around for a while?" She again didn't give him a chance to answer. "Good. But I can always find you back in Big Sky. If I need to."

He felt a chill run the length of his spine. All those days of feeling nothing but an emotional numbness were gone. Like a bucket of ice water poured over his head, he was now wide-awake as he realized what this woman was accusing him of—and Rachel, as well. She thought he was somehow involved in Humphrey's death? Because of a phone call?

With a silent groan, he thought about what had happened between him and Rachel at the wedding all those years ago. He hated to think of what the medical examiner would make of that.

Chapter Eight

Ford felt so shaken after his encounter with the medical examiner that he didn't go right to Rachel's room. Instead, he went outside and walked around town for a little while to clear his head. Big Timber was a small Western ranch town set in the middle of several impressive mountain ranges along the Yellowstone River.

The views would have taken his breath away if he wasn't already short of breath from what the medical examiner had accused him of doing. That he'd always wanted Rachel and had helped her kill her husband out of jealousy and was now her…defense? That was insane. How could she think such a thing?

By the time he returned to the hospital, he was still shaken but more in control. He'd come here to help Rachel. That Hitch—as she called herself—thought Rachel might have planned the whole thing so she could kill her husband was even crazier. Had the woman seen Rachel's face? The doctor had just taken her down to X-ray. Clearly, she'd been beaten.

If the medical examiner believed that was what had happened, then Rachel needed him even more than he'd thought. He had to see her again and he'd kept her waiting long enough. But he felt off balance as he found the doctor and got permission. The guard at the door let him in. As he stuck his head around the corner into her room, he did his best not to let her see how upset he was. He wondered how much of it was guilt over what had happened all those years ago.

"The doctor said you can have some company for a few minutes."

She waved him in. "I must look awful," Rachel said and touched the bandage at her cheek.

"You couldn't possibly look awful and you know it," Ford said as he pulled up the chair next to her bed. "Since you're fishing for compliments, you must be feeling better."

She chuckled even though it seemed to cause her pain. "That's what I always loved about you, Ford. You tell it to me straight." Her expression softened and he felt a slight electrical charge in the room. It was dated and weak, but still he felt it. "I'm so sorry." She began to cry. "The sheriff told me that I called you and that you…heard. I can hardly face you. Now I've involved you in all this."

"Rachel, really, it's all right."

"No, it's not. I never wanted anyone to know and now…"

He reached for her hand, thinking they all had things that they never wanted anyone to know. "When I got your call, it caught me at a really low point. The truth is, Rachel, your call saved my life."

She wiped her eyes. "Ford, you don't have to say that."

"I'm not." He hesitated, but only for a moment. "When you called, I was driving toward the edge of a cliff. I'd planned to end it."

Her blue eyes widened. "No," she said, looking horrified.

He nodded. "But then you called. So I'm the one who should be thanking you."

She studied him for a long moment and then laughed. "Look at us. Who would have ever thought this is where we would end up." He squeezed her hand.

For so long he hadn't felt anything and thought he never would again. Yet when he'd gotten her phone call yesterday and realized who it was, he'd felt as if his numbed emotions had been touched with a cattle prod. He'd known he had to come to Big Timber. Her wrong number had brought him back into her life. If that wasn't fate, he didn't know what was.

After his interview with the medical examiner, it was clear that Rachel needed him—even if she didn't know it yet. "How are you doing?" he asked.

"You've been through something like it, so I suspect you know."

He did know. Their situations were nothing alike except for the feeling of horror at where life had landed them. He hated to think what she must be going through. Seeing her again, it felt as if no time had passed since they last saw each other. He wanted to ask if she'd been happy at least some of those years with Humphrey, but didn't want to remind her about her marriage. She must have loved her husband. At least until the abuse began.

"Do you want to talk about it?" he asked.

She shook her head. "He just wasn't the man I thought he was. I really thought when we married that we would live happily ever after. Silly, huh?"

"I think that's the way most people go into a marriage."

Rachel picked at the edge of the sheet, her eyes downcast. "He was so sweet, so caring, so generous. At first." She looked up. "You know, he bought the ranch because of you."

"That's what his father told me." Ford remembered what Shyla had told him about how miserable Rachel had been at the ranch. Bart had even wanted to blame Ford for Humphrey's buying the ranch and dying here.

"Bart's here?" she said, her voice breaking. "You know, he hates me. Always has. He'll do everything in his power to get me sent to prison for life."

"We won't let that happen."

Eyes shiny and bright, she smiled up at him, taking him back to that day in college—those few precious moments in the park before she saw Humphrey.

HITCH HAD WATCHED Ford Cardwell from the hospital window as he'd left earlier. He'd had his hands in the pockets of his jeans, his head down. She'd obviously upset him. Because it hadn't been true? Or because it had?

She had seen how anxious he'd been earlier to see Rachel Collinwood. At the window, she'd decided to wait him out, knowing he would be back once he'd calmed down. The fact that he'd been so upset told her how deep his feelings apparently went for the woman in question. Sure enough, he'd come back and gone straight to Rachel's room.

From down the hall, she now watched him exit the woman's room. It was time to take this to the next step. Hitch put in a call to the sheriff, then headed down the hall toward Rachel Collinwood's room. As she walked, she mentally processed what she'd learned from Ford

Cardwell. If Rachel needed someone she could depend on, well, then she'd certainly made the right call—so to speak—when she'd hit Ford Cardwell's number.

Hitch pushed open the hospital room door, already knowing what she was going to find. Still, she stepped in and stood for a moment studying Rachel, who lay in her bed, eyes closed. Hitch was curious what kind of woman inspired the kind of loyalty the flyboy hero had for her.

Rachel Westlake Collinwood even in her current condition radiated that kind of beauty that few women possessed. Though bruised, lacerated and swollen, her face still had the heart shape so popular on magazine covers. The woman's eyes, she knew from her online search, were big and deep blue. Those eyes now opened in surprise to find Hitch studying her with speculation. Hitch saw the woman's guard come up. Had the sheriff warned her about the female medical examiner?

"Rachel Collinwood?" she said, stepping to the bed. "I'm state medical examiner Henrietta 'Hitch' Roberts." She pulled up a chair beside the bed. "I need to ask you a few questions about what happened yesterday. You don't mind if I video this." She set up her phone so it was aimed directly at the woman, not waiting for her approval. "So, Mrs. Collinwood, why don't you tell me in your own words exactly how this all happened. I know the sheriff already took your statement. You don't mind going through it for me, though, do you, just for the record?"

Rachel glanced at the phone, then at Hitch. Her eyes instantly filled with tears. "He's dead, isn't he?"

Hitch met her watery gaze. "He is. Why don't we start with what happened before you got home." She caught that moment of surprise, just a flash in the woman's eyes. Rachel hadn't mentioned that she'd just gotten home from town when she'd been questioned by the sheriff.

"Or do you want to start with the argument that began before the two of you returned to the ranch?" Hitch asked.

Rachel Collinwood swallowed and seemed to be buying time. "This is very hard to talk about. I've suspected for some time that my husband's been having an affair. When he said he had to go into town to pick up some part or another, I followed him. I caught up with him outside the woman's house and we argued. I went home, upset, and he followed me."

From there, Hitch noticed that this was the same story she'd told the sheriff on video, almost verbatim. She'd learned that interrupting the speaker often changed their account because they were so used to telling it in order, they would forget where they were. She didn't intend to get the same exact story from Rachel Collinwood if she could help it.

"That two-lane highway into town doesn't get much traffic," Hitch said, stopping the flow of the woman's words. "It must have been difficult to follow him into town since he would know your vehicle."

"I took the pickup. I figured he'd expect me to take my car."

"Your car being…"

"The BMW. Anyway…" She picked up her water glass next to the bed, adjusted the straw and took a sip. "When I got home, I heard him coming. He'd been angry in town. I was suddenly afraid for my life."

"Why would you go back to the house if he'd physically abused you before?"

"He had, but never like…that day," she said, dropping her gaze to her hands lying on the sheet as she toyed with the space where her wedding bands had been. The hospital staff normally removed jewelry for safekeeping. But in this case, the DCI investigators had taken all of her jewelry as evidence.

"But you had to be expecting trouble, right? Otherwise, why carry the gun in your purse? Unless you planned to kill him."

The woman's gaze shot up to hers in surprise. "I…I want a lawyer. And turn that thing off." She made a swipe at the phone, but Hitch got hold of it before Rachel could knock it to the floor. "I have nothing more to say to you. You're trying to twist my words. After everything I've been through, I can't believe…" She glared at Hitch. "I would think another woman would understand. He could have killed me! He would have, too, if I hadn't…" She clamped her lips shut and looked away. "Please go. I have nothing more to say to you."

"I need to inform you that you are under arrest pending the results of this investigation and a possible trial," Hitch said. "Once you are able to leave the hospital, you will be taken into custody until a hearing before a judge, in which case you will either be allowed bail or put behind bars."

"You can't be serious!" the woman cried. "He would have *killed* me. He told me he was going to kill me!"

"In the meantime, you will be fitted for an ankle bracelet that requires you to stay on this floor of the hospital." Hitch pocketed her phone as she heard the sheriff talking to the guard outside the room. "If you'll excuse me for a moment," she said and stepped out.

The sheriff lumbered toward her looking angry and upset.

"Sheriff, I need you to inform Mrs. Collinwood of her rights and make sure she understands she is under arrest for the death of her husband."

"That's why you got me down here?" he demanded angrily. "You got me away from my lunch for this?" He shook his head. "You are one heartless woman."

"I'm just doing my job. Isn't that proper procedure in a domestic homicide? I see no reason to let this run the full seventy-two hours. Mrs. Collinwood has admitted to shooting her husband with the intent to kill. Sheriff, if you prefer, I can call—"

The man growled. "I don't need you calling anyone," he snapped.

Minutes later, after the sheriff had read Mrs. Collinwood her rights, she was fitted with an ankle bracelet. Hitch stood at the door and watched. Rachel Collinwood lay in the bed, her face turned to the wall, quietly crying.

Hitch's cell phone rang. She took it on the way out of the hospital.

"I thought you'd want to know. Two shots were fired from the weapon that killed Humphrey Collinwood," Bradley from DCI told her.

She stopped just short of her SUV. "How many casings did you find?"

"Only one in the kitchen on the floor."

"Were there any slugs found in the wall?" she asked, frowning as she tried to understand when and where the other shot might have been fired.

"Negative. But both shots had been fired close to the same time."

Hitch swore under her breath. "We have to find that other slug and casing."

"Have you seen the size of that ranch?" he asked.

"Let me see what I can do. That casing is somewhere out there, and I have a theory that the first shot was a practice one."

Chapter Nine

Hitch couldn't get the news off her mind as she drove out to the Collinwood Ranch. Pulling up to the house, she thought she saw movement inside but realized it was only the reflection of the crime scene tape flickering in the breeze.

After getting out of her SUV, she stepped under that tape and entered the house with the code the sheriff had given her. The first thing that struck her was the absolute silence, followed almost instantly by the smell of cleaning supplies.

The kitchen shone white—all signs of the violence gone. She stepped in and looked around. The DCI unit had been thorough; she didn't doubt that. Which meant the second casing hadn't been in this room. Just as the slug wasn't embedded in any of the walls. Glancing around, though, she knew that the other shot hadn't been fired in here.

Her gaze went to the sliding glass door from the kitchen out onto the deck. She carefully opened the door. The breeze brought the sweet scent of pine and summer as she stepped out. Had Rachel stood here, with the gun in her hand? Rachel Collinwood wasn't the kind of woman who left things to chance, right?

Because of that, she would fire the gun to make sure it worked. To know how it felt, how much it kicked in her hand, what it would do when the time came.

Hitch walked to the edge of the deck and leaned her elbow on the railing to take aim. She spotted the closest pine tree and pretended to fire. Then she glanced down at the thick shrubbery below. The weapon would have ejected the casing.

But before Hitch went digging in the shrubs, she wanted a look at that pine.

A dozen yards from the deck, she stopped in front of the tree. She didn't see it at first. The bullet hadn't skinned much of the bark. Instead, it had lodged in the soft wood and was nearly covered by a piece of bark. She walked back to her vehicle for her satchel, took a few photographs, then pulled on latex gloves and went to work with her pocketknife.

As the slug came out, she dropped it into an evidence bag. Hitch told herself that anyone could have fired the weapon from the deck. But Bradley had said the two shots had been fired close together.

Holding the slug up in the sunlight, she knew it didn't prove that Rachel had orchestrated the murder of her husband. But then again, it did add to growing evidence that she had.

Putting down her satchel, she bent at the edge of the deck. If she found the empty casing... She had been looking in the shrubbery directly off the deck railing when something farther back under the deck, closer to the house, caught her eye. The casing lay next to the house and the door out to the deck.

Goose bumps rippled over her skin. She'd thought that Rachel had taken the first shot as target practice so she knew how the gun would react when she pulled the trigger. She would have put her elbows on the railing to take aim because she wasn't used to firing this weapon.

But Hitch knew now that it didn't happen that way. Rachel Collinwood had fired the shot that hit the tree standing at the open kitchen doorway. She had practiced with the gun long before the day of the shooting.

It explained why Humphrey Collinwood's voice was never heard on the phone call to Ford. Because he was already dead from the first shot fired—before Rachel had "accidentally" made that alleged pocket dial.

While Humphrey Collinwood lay in a pool of his own blood, his wife had taken the phone, made the call, acted out the attack and then stepped to the open glass doors and fired the shot that Ford heard before she'd disconnected and called 911.

That would explain why Ford Cardwell hadn't heard Humphrey Collinwood say a word.

After taking a photo of where the casing had landed in relation to the house, Hitch put her camera away to leave. But as she did, she felt an icy chill and turned quickly, unable to shake the feeling that someone was watching her. Her gaze took in the sliding glass door into the kitchen. For a moment, she'd expected to see someone standing there.

But the doorway was empty. So was the yard. So was the land that ran from the house to the rolling hills to the mountains in the distance. Behind her, the breeze stirred the boughs of the pine tree, making an eerie moaning sound.

Hitch laughed at her foolishness, but it sounded hollow. She didn't spook easily, but this wasn't the first time she'd felt…something that raised goose bumps across her skin. She doubted it would be the last, given her job. And yet, as she climbed back into her SUV to leave, she found herself staring at the house, unable to shake what felt like a warning.

WHEN FORD VISITED Rachel again later that afternoon at the hospital, he was glad to see that she seemed in better spirits. Her face was badly bruised, but several of the bandages had come off. Also, she seemed glad to see him.

"You look as if you're feeling better," he said, going to her bedside.

"Looks can be deceiving," she said, meeting his gaze. "I'm scared, Ford. I'm under arrest."

"My uncle's a marshal in Big Sky. I talked to him earlier. He said that it's police procedure. What does your lawyer say?"

"That we'll fight it. The problem, he says, is that self-defense claims are fairly common. Because of the amount of force I used…well, it could complicate things. If I hadn't killed him, only wounded him…" She met his gaze. "He was so close. I knew that if he got his hands on me again…" She looked down at her own hands knotted together on top of the sheet. "I was holding the gun. You heard me tell him not to come any closer or I would shoot him." She closed her eyes. "He wouldn't listen. I had no choice. I pulled the trigger."

He placed his hand over hers, surprised someone had told her not only that she'd accidentally called him, but also what he'd heard her say before the gunshot. "What can I do to help you?"

Rachel opened her eyes and wiped them before she turned that high-wattage smile on him. And he'd been so certain just forty-eight hours ago that he'd never be able to feel again. There was a time that her smile would have filled him with so much joy. He told himself the reason he didn't feel that joy now, couldn't because of everything that had happened to them both. He realized Rachel was still talking.

"I don't know what I would have done if you hadn't been here," she was saying. "It's crazy, it's like fate, but I'm so thankful that somehow I hit your number. What are the odds?"

What were the odds? he thought.

"So just your being here is enough," Rachel said. "I can't tell you what it means to me."

"I'm sure your lawyer will get you bail and fight this," he assured her.

"I don't know. He says we have to prove that I was defending myself and believed I was in imminent danger."

"Your injuries should prove that."

She nodded. "It's just hard to prove when there was only the two of us there." She brightened. "But I guess it wasn't just me and Humphrey. You were there." She looked away. "I can't believe any of this is happening."

He knew the feeling. "How is your head?"

She grimaced. "It hurts. The pain pills help. I can't believe what he did to me." She began to cry. "The doctor is releasing me tomorrow, and if I don't make bail, I'm going to jail."

"Do you have money for bail?"

She nodded. "I was afraid all our assets might have been frozen until the outcome of the investigation. But thankfully, they weren't. The thing is, Humphrey always handled the money. I have no idea how much I will be able to raise."

"I'll help what I can," he said.

"I know." She flashed him that smile again. "I knew I could count on you. Oh, Ford." She took his hand in her two. "I'll never be able to thank you enough."

"I should have known you would be here," said a female voice behind him. He turned to see Shyla come into the hospital room. She moved to the bed to give Rachel an awkward hug and a kiss on the cheek. "How's our girl?"

Ford looked to Rachel and smiled. "She's doing okay, under the circumstances." A silence fell over the room. "I'll leave you two alone so you can visit."

"Don't run off on my account," Shyla said, even though he got the feeling that she was anxious to talk to Rachel alone. Because she would be more honest with her than she'd been with him?

He realized that he was letting Hitch get to him, her and her suspicions. "I've got to go anyway," he said, as if there was anywhere he needed to be. But maybe he should see how much money he could raise on Rachel's behalf if she needed more bail money. "But I'll be back."

Rachel grabbed his wrist as he started to turn away. "Thank you," she whispered.

Ford stepped out into the hall, closing the hospital room door behind him. He stood in the hallway for a moment. Why had this visit with Rachel left him feeling…not so sure of her? The medical examiner had him questioning everything Rachel said, and he hated her for doing that to him. He shook his head and reached into his pocket for his pickup keys. Empty.

He swore under his breath and turned back to Rachel's room, remembering putting them down on the side table when she spilled her water.

But as he pushed open the door, he froze as he overheard Rachel's words. "I should have married Ford." He started to ease the door closed and stopped.

Shyla laughed. "Oh, please. He wasn't even in the running and you know it. His father owns a barbecue joint with his brothers."

"They have a dozen barbecue joints, as you call them, and were worth a bunch even back in college."

"You ran a financial on him?"

Rachel's laugh was like a fingernail down a blackboard. "Why does that surprise you?"

"Actually, nothing you do surprises me," Shyla said. "I know you, Rach. Ford told me how you two met. A squirrel? Really. You just happened to be there feeding a squirrel? You went after Humphrey and you used Ford to do it."

Silence, then Rachel's voice, stronger than it had been when she was talking to him earlier. "I wanted to marry someone who could take care of me in the way I wanted to become accustomed. What's wrong with that?"

"*Really?* Have you noticed how that turned out? You're on your way to jail when you get out of here."

"Maybe. We'll see. I'll make bail. Ford's going to help me."

"Of course he is."

Ford saw his chance and said "I forgot my keys!" as he pushed the door all the way open. Both women turned in surprise as he hurried in, grabbed his keys and waved an apologetic goodbye as he left again.

He reached the door and stopped just out of their

sight around the corner at the edge of the hallway. The deputy was no longer outside her door since she'd been fitted with an ankle bracelet. Ford didn't let the door quite close.

"Do you think he heard us?"

Shyla laughed. "Even if he did hear, Ford's still so in love with you he'd forgive you anything. Oh, don't give me that look. This comes as no surprise to you. So tell me. How is it that you just happened to call his number?"

"I have no idea. But he saved my life."

Ford closed the door softly behind him. He stood in the hall trying to catch his breath. His stomach roiled with what he'd heard. He tried to still it, assuring himself that he hadn't heard anything he hadn't already known. He'd seen how Rachel felt about money even back in college. She'd been at the university on loans and small scholarships. She'd hated being poor and had made no bones about it.

Yet he couldn't help but think about the medical examiner's suspicions. He felt sick to his stomach. Worse, Hitch thought he and Rachel had planned this whole thing to get rid of her husband. He'd come running to save her—even though he hadn't forgotten what had happened at her wedding.

What had she gotten him involved in this time? Murder?

Chapter Ten

Hitch decided since she was already at the ranch that she would see if she could find the hired hands. If Rachel Collinwood was being abused by her husband, then someone must have noticed.

According to the sheriff, the Collinwoods employed only two young men who lived in the old ranch house several miles from their employers' home.

As she approached, she could see horses in a pasture and a corral and several outbuildings next to a large barn. The house was a modest two-story farmhouse with a wide porch complete with a swing. Hitch wondered about the former owners of the ranch. Had they moved to Arizona? One of them died? Why had they sold to the Collinwoods? Often it was because there was no one who wanted to keep the place and work it. But in this case, maybe they'd been made an offer they just couldn't refuse.

Hitch parked in front of the house, and before she could get out, two young men headed toward her from the direction of the barn.

Both men appeared to be in their early twenties, tall and gangly and green behind the ears. She introduced herself. The more handsome of the pair was Pete Baxter. He was also the more cocky of the two. Clayton Mandeville was the more talkative of the two.

"So what does a state medical examiner do?" Clayton asked, grinning. "Cut up dead bodies?"

"That and investigate for the state," she said. In this case, she had been given carte blanche from the governor. Which was flattering, but she could feel the weight of it on her shoulders. The message had been clear: don't screw this up. "Can we step inside and talk for a few minutes?"

The house was homey, though dated. Once seated in the living room, she asked, "So the two of you live here?" They nodded. "What is it you do here on the ranch?"

Pete laughed. "We look after things."

"Does the ranch run cattle?"

"It's not a real ranch, if that's what you're asking," Clayton said. "The only animals are the horses."

"I saw a tractor out there," Hitch said. "Does the ranch grow anything?"

They shook their heads. "So you basically take care of how many horses?"

"Six. When the boss wants to ride, we saddle one of them up for him," Clayton said. "We muck out stalls and exercise the horses."

She nodded, looking from one man to the other. Clearly, they had a pretty good setup here. "What about Mrs. Collinwood? Does she ride?" They both shook their heads. "So you don't see her often?" More head shakes. "Where were the two of you yesterday?"

"We had the day off," Clayton said without hesitation.

"Was it your usual day off?"

She asked the question of Clayton, who scratched his neck before saying, "I had some extra time coming. The missus told me to go ahead and take it off."

She looked to Pete, who added, "It was my regular day off."

"So you were both here at the house?"

Clayton shook his head. "I went into town for a while. We were out of a few things."

"He went to see his girlfriend," Pete said with a chuckle.

"And you?" she asked Pete.

"I was here all day. I took one of the horses out for a while and then did chores since someone has to muck out the stalls." He elbowed Clayton.

"So you usually both don't have the same day off. Why yesterday?"

Pete shrugged. "Clayton wanted to see his girlfriend. I didn't mind filling in for him. It isn't like we have a lot to do around here."

"So the Collinwoods don't really know what the two of you do here," she said and hesitated since she wasn't sure how to ask the next question. "Have either of you seen any trouble between Mr. and Mrs. Collinwood?"

Clayton started to speak, but Pete cut him off. "We shouldn't be talking about our employers," Pete said.

"One of them is dead and the other arrested," Hitch pointed out. "I'm not sure how long you're going to be employed. What I need to know is if you had reason to see the two of them together since she didn't ride any of the horses."

"We'd get called up to the house sometimes to do a chore for the missus," Clayton said.

"Did you hear them fighting? Ever see him hit her?"

"Never," Clayton said quickly. "They argued. You know, like old married couples do. Like my parents. He got annoyed with her, but I could tell he loved her. Can't see him raising his hand to her, though."

She looked to Pete, who was studying his boots. "You disagree?"

"I don't like telling tales out of school, but I'd seen her a few times in tears and noticed some bruises on her. I also saw him looking at her a few times like he wanted to kill her."

She studied the ranch hand, curious why his story was so different from Clayton's. "*Like he wanted to kill her?* What kind of look is that?"

Pete shrugged. "You'd know it if you saw it."

"So what happened yesterday doesn't surprise you?" she asked, sure they both had heard all about it.

Pete shook his head. "Not everyone can take living out here in the middle of nowhere. She wasn't raised for this kind of living. Like her husband cared."

Hitch could hear the sympathy in his words. It was clear which side he was on. "She ever talk to you about how she felt?" He looked at his boots again, confirming it. Rachel had complained to the older of the hired hands, the one closer to her own age. There was nothing illegal about that—unless she needed his sympathy for when she killed her husband. Or worse, had been hoping to get him to help her.

"Well, it shocked *me* what happened," Clayton was saying. "I can't imagine what might have set that off, but I never thought he'd do something like that, let alone her ever shoot him. I would have doubted that she even knew how to fire a gun."

Pete merely stared at his boots and said nothing more.

As Hitch drove away from the ranch, she considered the differences between their opinions. Rachel had gone to Pete with her complaints about living on the ranch—and about Humphrey. But Pete didn't seem like the type she would trust as her accomplice. He seemed to Hitch like the kind of man who would have bled her dry for the rest of her life.

That was what had been bothering her, Hitch realized. Rachel couldn't have pulled this off without help. But who had she turned to? She needed a man who was more than sympathetic. She needed one who'd get involved with murder.

She thought about the man who'd allegedly come running the moment he heard the gunshot, Ford Cardwell. After pulling onto the two-lane paved highway, she hadn't gone far when she looked back and saw a pickup behind her. It had one of those large cattle guard grilles on the front. With the sun glinting off the windshield, she couldn't see the driver at this distance. Had the pickup come from the Collinwood Ranch? She didn't think so. Wouldn't she have noticed if either Pete or Clayton had followed her?

The pickup appeared to be the same color as the one that had been sitting outside the morgue last night. She sped up. The pickup driver did the same. She slowed down. The pickup driver did the same.

She told herself that it didn't mean anything, but she was glad when she neared the outskirts of Big Timber and looked back to see the truck gone. It wasn't like her to feel this jumpy. But she couldn't remember ever having a case like this one. Since the first day on this case, she'd had a bad feeling she couldn't shake that things would get worse before they got better.

At the back of her mind was always that one big question. What if she was wrong? What if Humphrey Collinwood's death was exactly like what it appeared to be and Rachel Collinwood was innocent?

Her cell phone rang. She quickly picked up when she saw it was coming from the DCI lab.

"We found something interesting when we began checking the broken shards of glass and pottery found on the floor of the kitchen at the crime scene," Bradley told her. "Fingerprints."

She frowned. "*Fingerprints?* Of course there would be fingerprints."

"Yep, of the lady of the house. But what's missing are the fingerprints of the deceased. If he had broken up the kitchen—"

"You'd have found his fingerprints on the shards," she said and felt that light-headed feeling she always did when a case began to come together.

FORD HADN'T WANTED to go back to the hotel right away. He kept replaying what he'd heard Rachel and Shyla talking about. Rachel had planned the whole meeting with him—and Humphrey. She'd already staked out the man she planned to marry. That day with the squirrel… She must have known that he and Humphrey often came to that spot in the park after chem class. The woman had done her homework.

There was something so cold and calculating about that. He knew Rachel had been driven, but clearly there were things about her that he'd missed. He shook his head, feeling off balance. Was it possible she'd set this whole domestic homicide up for the money?

He refused to believe she would do something like

that even though he knew what money meant to her. Once at a party, the two of them had struck up a conversation outside. That was back when she'd smoked. He'd found her standing at the deck railing. When he'd joined her, he could see that she'd consumed more than she usually drank.

She'd opened up to him about growing up living hand to mouth and her fear of being poor. "My father used to call it the snake pit, saying it was hard for people like us to climb out. That we could never feel like we belonged, even if we made a whole lot of money. No one like us gets out of the snake pit, he used to say."

"Rachel," he'd said that night on the deck. "Look at you. You're going to an Ivy League university. Your father was wrong."

She'd looked at him with tears in her eyes. "Are you sure about that?" She'd scoffed. "What if we have to be born into a family like Humphrey's with real old wealth to ever be one of them?"

He'd forgotten about that conversation until now. Rachel had married into money, but had she still not felt as if she belonged or ever could?

"Ford?"

He turned to see Shyla come out of the hospital.

"Are you all right?" she asked, smiling oddly at him. "You were just standing here on the sidewalk as if you didn't know which way to go."

She was joking, but she had no idea how true that was.

"Just enjoying this beautiful day," he said.

Shyla lit up a cigarette. As she let out a cloud of smoke, a sheriff's department car pulled up. The deputy on the passenger side put down his window. "Hey, baby," the officer behind the wheel called. Ford couldn't see him without stooping down. He didn't. The officer on the passenger side was studying Ford openly and making him nervous. "We were just going to the drive-in for lunch. You wanna come?"

"Sure. I'll catch up to you." Shyla turned to Ford. "You want to join us?"

He declined and her husband took off, making the tires squeal on the cruiser. "You go on ahead. I have some things I need to do. I thought you said you were married to a cowboy?"

"Don't let the uniform fool you," she said with a laugh. "He's all cowboy. You should see his Wild West fast draw. He could be a movie star," she said as she stubbed out her cigarette on the sidewalk and headed toward her car.

Ford watched her go, wondering at how people changed. The lawless young woman who Rachel had bailed out of jail back in college had married a cop cowboy with a fast draw? He shook his head. Wasn't it possible that if Shyla could change, Humphrey could have turned into a man who'd tried to beat his wife to death?

Chapter Eleven

Hitch got the call from Lori Stevenson from DCI on the way back into town. "Those phone records you asked about? I'm emailing them to you. We're still checking out the numbers. Only one call jumped out at us. Didn't you tell us that Rachel Collinwood believed her husband was having an affair with a woman named Emily Sutton? Well, Mrs. Collinwood called her cell phone number at ten the morning of the shooting."

"She called before she went into town?" Hitch said, frowning. "How long was the call?"

"Four minutes."

"*Four minutes?* She wasn't simply checking to see if the woman was working. She'd actually talked to her that long?" Hitch had two quick thoughts. How had she gotten Emily's cell phone number? And why had Rachel left that part out of her statement? "Okay, thanks. Anything else?"

"Bart Collinwood wants his son's body so he can have him flown home and buried. He's called everyone, from what I can tell, including the governor."

Hitch was surprised the governor hadn't called her. Yet. "Great. I need to run a few more tests," she said. It wasn't quite true, but she wasn't ready to turn over the body. She had a feeling that she'd missed something. "I'll let Mr. Bart Collinwood know." She disconnected and drove to the morgue.

Once in the autopsy room, she pulled Humphrey Collinwood's body out of the cooler, that niggling feeling growing. She was certain the reason the deceased hadn't said a word during the fight was because he was already dead. But what if he was unable to speak for another reason? She began to search the body for injection marks.

THE SHERIFF STOOD at the foot of Rachel Collinwood's hospital bed, Stetson in hand. She was so pretty and sweet and looked so shattered and afraid. "I have some good news for you." At least he hoped she'd see it as that. "A bail hearing has been scheduled for tomorrow, the day of your hospital release. That means, if you can make bail, you won't have to even spend one night in my jail behind bars."

Her smile was weak, but it still warmed his heart. "Thank you so much, Sheriff. You've been so kind. I can't tell you how much I appreciate it. I know this is just standard procedure, that you aren't responsible for me being arrested."

"No," Charley quickly assured her. "I don't understand why a woman like yourself has to be put through this. It makes no sense to me. Anyone can see that you feared for your life. Justifiable use of force. That's what it was."

"Unfortunately, not everyone feels like you do. That woman, the medical examiner, for one."

"Hitch Roberts. I know," he said with a shake of his

head. "You'd think as a woman, she would be more understanding."

"My father-in-law is even worse. Not that I blame him. His son is dead, but he *raised* him. That's why Bart doesn't want to believe what really happened. It would reflect on him and the Collinwood name."

All the sheriff could do was nod for a few moments. "You got yourself a good lawyer?"

"I hope so. If I do get out on bail, will I be able to go back out to the ranch?"

"I don't see why not," Charley said. "They're through with your house. I had someone go out there and clean things up for you. I hope you don't mind."

"Sheriff, that is so sweet." Tears filled her eyes. "Thank you so much. That is so thoughtful. But I doubt I can ever go into that kitchen again."

"She never went in there much anyway," Bart Collinwood said behind the sheriff as he came into the room. "It wasn't like she was much of a wife to my son."

The sheriff turned on him. "I told you, you aren't allowed in here. I won't have you badgering this woman."

"You told me a lot of things, Sheriff, but I just talked to the governor and he said I have every right to face the woman who killed my son."

"In court. In the meantime…" Charley pulled out his phone to call Security as Collinwood took a step toward the bed.

"You will pay for what you did," Bart declared, pointing a finger at her. "If I have my way, you'll rot in prison."

"Security is on the way," the sheriff said. "Unless you want me to arrest you—"

"On what charge?" Bart demanded. "Anyway,

I'm leaving. I've had my say." He looked again at his daughter-in-law. "You might have fooled this local yokel with your crocodile tears, Rachel, but you have never fooled me. You married my son for the Collinwood money. I'll kill you myself before I'll let you spend a dime more of it."

With that, the man stormed out, pushing past the hospital security guard on his way through the door.

"I hope you heard that, Sheriff," Rachel said, her voice breaking. "He just threatened to kill me. Father like son." Then she burst into tears.

EMILY SUTTON SQUIRMED in the chair as the video recorder was turned on. She looked so young in her jeans and T-shirt. Hitch had asked to sit in on the interview with the waitress who was allegedly having an affair with Humphrey Collinwood.

The sheriff grumbled and complained but agreed. After introducing herself to Emily, Hitch had taken a seat and pulled out her notebook and pen.

"State your name and occupation," the sheriff said after giving the date and adding that the state medical examiner was also here.

As soon as Emily finished, he asked, "Were you having an affair with Humphrey Collinwood?"

Her eyes widened in alarm. "No." She shook her head adamantly. "We were just friends."

"Friends?" the sheriff asked mockingly.

Hitch shot him a warning look. "Would you please describe your friendship, Miss Sutton?"

"He came into the café a lot of mornings."

"Without his wife?" the sheriff said.

"He said she wasn't an early riser." Emily smiled.

"He said he liked to watch the sun rise and that he loved the café's waffles. He always ordered the same thing. He said his wife didn't cook."

"What else did he say about his wife?" Hitch asked.

Emily shook her head and looked away for a moment. "Nothing bad. He just seemed...lonely. I got the impression he needed someone to talk to." She smiled. "I'm a good listener."

"You aren't going to tell me that he didn't talk about his wife, are you?" the sheriff said, ignoring Hitch's look.

"It wasn't like he complained about her. He didn't. I just got the feeling that they didn't have a lot in common. He'd been looking for a horse for her birthday. She loved pintos and paints. My cousin up in Malta raises them, so I put him in touch with Tom."

"We'll need your cousin's contact information," Hitch said.

"I can give it to you. He'll tell you."

"Did Mr. Collinwood buy a horse for his wife's birthday?" Hitch asked. "I understand she didn't ride much."

"He did," Emily said. "He showed me a photograph. It's a beautiful horse. He was hoping that his wife would love it and that they could ride together. He'd hoped it would encourage her to ride more."

"Humphrey ever come over to your house?" the sheriff said, drawing her attention to him again.

"Just to drop off a thank-you present, that's all. It was my day off and he said he had to fly out the next day for a board meeting. He wouldn't even come inside."

"What did he give you?" Hitch asked.

She beamed, clearly pleased with the gift. "It was a miniature carousel. I'd mentioned once that one of my happiest memories was riding a paint horse on a carousel." She blushed, her joy in the gift from Humphrey reddening her cheeks.

Hitch studied her for a moment, seeing her embarrassment and so much more. "You liked him."

She nodded. "He was nice. He reminded me of my father." She looked to the sheriff. "My father died in Afghanistan. He was a marine."

"You more than liked Humphrey Collinwood," the sheriff said.

Her head came up, eyes widening. "No. He was just nice to me. He was married. He would never have…" She shook her head and lowered it again. "He told me how much he loved his wife. That's why he wanted to surprise her with the horse. He said he was trying to find a way to make her happy in Montana."

"Tell me about the phone call you got from his wife, Rachel Collinwood," Hitch said, surprising both Emily and the sheriff. "She called you the morning of the shooting."

Emily nodded, tears in her eyes. "She thought we were having an affair. I told her we weren't, but she wouldn't listen. She was upset and wouldn't believe me." She paused for a moment. Then said, "Tell me that isn't what they argued about, what…got him killed."

"It wasn't," Hitch said before the sheriff could speak. "You aren't to blame." She stood. "I think we've heard enough."

"Maybe he didn't have an affair with the waitress, but he wanted to," the sheriff argued after Emily Sutton left and Hitch had returned from making a call out in the hallway.

Hitch shook her head at him. "You heard her. Humphrey Collinwood loved his wife. He was buying her a horse for her birthday. I called Emily's cousin. Humphrey Collinwood paid for the horse. It was going to be delivered on his wife's birthday next week. Does that sound like a man who's having an affair?"

The sheriff clearly refused to give an inch. "Sounds like a guilty conscience to me."

Hitch sighed and left before she said something she'd regret.

Back in her hotel room, she watched the videos the sheriff had sent her again of both Ford Cardwell's statement and then Rachel Collinwood's. She was even more suspicious of why Humphrey Collinwood hadn't said a word during the altercation. Ford had heard only Rachel's voice. It was almost as if the husband hadn't been there. And yet she hadn't found any needle marks on the body.

"What are we looking for?" the lab tech asked when Hitch called to request more tests to be run on the samples.

"Run the whole drug spectrum," she told her. There had to be a reason Humphrey Collinwood hadn't spoken at all during the time Ford had been listening in on the alleged pocket-dialed phone call. If he wasn't already dead, then he had to have been drugged or incapacitated in some way.

"Can you put a rush on it?" Hitch asked. "I'm worried that my suspect will make bail tomorrow and that might be the last time we ever see her."

"You're that sure she's a flight risk?"

"If she thinks she might be doing time, she'll run."

The lab tech asked, "Anything in particular you're thinking you're going to find?"

"Something that would debilitate a two-hundred-pound male. Or possibly enrage one. I'm betting it's the first—if there was a drug in his system at the time of his death. Look for something…unusual." Rachel wouldn't have used anything she thought would show up in a normal drug sample taken during the autopsy.

"That is the whole spectrum," the lab tech said with a laugh. "I'll see what I can do."

Hitch disconnected and sighed. She doubted she was going to be able to sleep. She'd talked to the doctor earlier. Rachel Collinwood would be released from the hospital and arraigned tomorrow. If the judge gave her bail, then the woman would be free. Rich, as well. The judge would confiscate her passport, but any fool knew how easy it would be for a woman with her resources to get one in another name and slip the loop.

Except Hitch was determined that wasn't going to happen if she had anything to do with it.

The question was, where did Ford Cardwell fit into all this once Rachel was free?

She'd seen the haunted look in his eyes. After what he'd been through, what was it doing to him being this involved with an old flame suspected of murder?

Hitch guessed she would know tomorrow. What would Ford do once Rachel was out on bail? Go back to Big Sky? He was Rachel's defense, her proof that she feared for her life. Would she want to keep him around? Now that he'd given his statement to law enforcement, she really didn't need him anymore.

All Hitch's instincts told her that the woman was

through with Ford. He'd played his part and now he needed to walk away. But would he? It would depend on how deep he was in all this.

Either way, if Hitch was right, Ford was in a very dangerous place. She wondered if he was beginning to realize it. Pulling out her phone, she called his cell phone number.

"It's state medical examiner Henrietta Roberts. Hitch? Where are you?"

It seemed to take him a moment, as if he had to place her name. "At the hospital."

Of course he was, she thought. "I need to talk to you again."

"It's late. Can't this—"

"No, it can't wait," she said. "I'm on my way. How about we meet in the waiting room on Mrs. Collinwood's floor?"

It took her longer to get there than she'd planned. When Hitch pushed open the door to the waiting room, she stopped cold with the realization that she'd caught Ford in an unguarded moment. He looked so miserable that she knew instinctively that it had more than something to do with this case. She couldn't imagine the trauma he'd gone through when he was overseas with the military. She knew a little about survivor's remorse and wondered if that wasn't playing a part in this.

Did she still believe that he'd been in on this with Rachel? The woman had needed an accomplice to pull it off. She hadn't beaten herself and neither had Humphrey Collinwood. Whoever had helped her kill her husband had to be as cold-blooded as she was. Or he'd gotten himself into something he now regretted. As miserable as Ford looked, she feared he might be that man.

Right now, sitting there in this room alone, he looked like what she realized he was. A broken man. Her heart hurt for him. She wanted to go to him, take him in her arms, mend every broken part of him. The emotions surprised her, especially with him so deeply involved in this case.

But she pushed those emotions down. She had to come at him again. It felt cruel, but she had to do her job. He was involved one way or another. Maybe it had only been when Rachel had "accidentally" called him in the middle of her life-and-death situation. Or maybe long before that.

Either way, Hitch had to get to the truth.

She cleared her voice and Ford looked up, a shield coming back up as he quickly rose to his feet. "Why don't we step into the doctor's office again? It will be more private."

He looked as if he'd rather have a root canal, but he came with her.

Again, she turned on her phone to record their interview. After she'd entered the date, time and who was in the room, she said, "I'll tell you what's bothering me. It must be bothering you, too. Why didn't Humphrey speak during the phone call?"

"I have no idea, like I told you. The call wasn't that long."

"It was actually longer than you think. During that time, the only voice you heard was Rachel's. Where were you again when you got the call?"

"I was up in the mountains." He glanced away. He was definitely hiding something.

"What were you doing in the mountains? Hiking, fishing—"

"Just driving around. It's been a long time since I've been back in Montana. I just needed some time to myself."

"So you were alone." A nod. "What was your first thought when you heard—" she checked her notes "—a scream?"

He seemed to think about it. "I realized it was a woman in trouble, but I had no idea who it was. I hadn't checked to see who the call was from. I tried to get her to answer me."

"But she never did?"

"That's when I realized it must have been a pocket dial."

Hitch gave it a minute. "You didn't recognize her voice?" He shook his head. "Once you heard her say her husband's name, you must have been shocked."

"More than you can know," he said. "I couldn't believe it was Rachel and that the man she was begging not to hurt her was Humphrey. I still can't believe it."

"Neither can I," Hitch agreed. "What would you say is your relationship to Mrs. Collinwood?"

"I don't have a relationship with her."

"Because you hadn't seen or talked to either of them for fifteen years, since their wedding, right?"

"No. Not until we reconnected through social media a few weeks ago." He looked as if he wanted to say more but had stopped himself.

She raised a brow. "I believe you said in your statement that he was your best friend, and yet the three of you went fifteen years without talking or seeing each other. Something must have happened. Did he realize you were in love with his wife?"

He opened his mouth, closed it and opened it again. "Are we back to this?"

"You dropped everything to come running when she needed you. This sounds like your feelings run deeper than that of an old friend from college whom you hadn't even been in contact with for fifteen years."

His laugh was edged with bitterness. "I didn't have a lot going on when I got the call."

"You still care about her."

"That's not a crime. Look, she called *me*. Check her phone records. I was miles from here."

"Can you prove that?"

He started to say something but stopped and shook his head. "I told you. I was up in the mountains outside Big Sky."

"Did anyone see you?" she asked.

"Not that I know of."

"Then you raced here to save a woman who you hadn't seen in fifteen years."

"If you must know, she saved me." He looked away, then met her gaze. She saw his jaw muscles bunch. "I was about to drive off a cliff." He must have seen her shock. "I'm apparently suffering with PTSD—at least I have all of the symptoms. It was stupid and I regret even considering what I almost did. But I was only yards from the edge of the cliff, driving too fast in my pickup, when I got the call." He exhaled gruffly. "Happy?"

For a moment, she didn't know what to say. "You think she saved your life."

"That's what I thought at the time." He shook his head. "I don't know if I would have hit the brakes or not if my phone hadn't rung." He looked away again.

"I'm sorry." She realized this explained so much. If he thought she'd saved his life that day… "Do you still feel that she saved your life?"

"I don't know how I feel. All of this…" He raked a hand through his hair.

"Do you deny you have feelings for Rachel Collinwood?"

He chuckled. "I care what happens to her. But none of that has anything to do with what happened. I told you. I only recently reconnected with Rachel. That's how she had my number."

"When was the last time you reconnected with Mr. Collinwood?"

He looked down at his feet. "Years ago, just like I told you."

"At their wedding?"

He nodded, a muscle in his jaw tightening.

There was something there she couldn't put her finger on. Whatever had happened at the wedding, though, was the key. "When you and Mrs. Collinwood reconnected recently, did she mention any conflict in her marriage?"

"It wasn't that kind of *reconnection*," he said. "We didn't share anything more personal than phone numbers."

"She was the one who contacted you? So you're on social media."

"One of my nieces insisted on signing me up. I hardly pay any attention to it."

"Until you saw a friend request from Rachel. But after you shared your number, you didn't call her?"

"No. I doubt I would have. She was married and a lot of water had flowed under that bridge."

Hitch nodded, confirming her suspicions about whatever had happened at the wedding. But did it pertain to the murder? It could be simply because Ford Cardwell had never gotten over the woman and had to distance himself from the two of them. Had Rachel known about his crush on her? Of course, Hitch thought. That was why she'd called him. "But here you are, coming to her defense."

"I came here to tell the sheriff what I heard during the phone call, that's all."

"You also said you came to Big Timber to make sure Rachel was all right."

When he didn't answer, she stared him down until he said, "Why are you trying to make something more out of this than it is?"

"Because Humphrey Collinwood is dead and I want to know why." She studied him openly for a moment.

He sighed, sounding worn out. "I want to know, as well. Maybe I want to know more than even you do. But other than the phone call, that's my only involvement in all this."

She wondered if he actually believed that. "Have you ever heard of a case of domestic homicide involving a husband's shooting where the wife put the gun outside the house because she was afraid he would use it on her?"

"I'm not familiar with any domestic homicide cases," he said impatiently.

"The wife got off because it appeared she hadn't planned to kill him. And yet she ran outside, knowing the gun was there."

Ford shook his head. "You really do think that Rachel took a beating so she could kill her husband. That would mean that she set this all up."

She heard something in his voice. The idea wasn't a new one for him. He was wondering the same thing, but afraid to admit it. "Humphrey Collinwood is a very wealthy man, but I think you know that. Did you also know that Rachel signed a prenuptial agreement that she couldn't benefit from that wealth if they divorced?"

"I didn't know anything about their…marriage arrangements."

"Dead, she walks away with everything the two have accumulated since the marriage, which is no small amount. Had she divorced him, she could have gotten half of whatever their high-priced lawyers didn't take. In other words, a whole lot less, and it could have been years before she got her share if there was a long legal battle, since his business is tied up with his father's."

She watched him grind his teeth but he said nothing. "Here's what bothers me. Other than the huge coincidence of her pocket dialing you in particular, you didn't hear him threatening her on the phone. Normally in an argument like the one you thought you overheard, the husband would have been saying something as he attacked his wife. Also, why did she have the gun with her in the kitchen? If she was really afraid for her life, why not leave? Why not call 911? Because she needed him dead to get the money."

He shook his head. "What if it was exactly what it seems and Humphrey was beating her?"

"Do you really believe that?"

"I don't know what to believe, but I'm starting to wonder if Bart got to you. He wants his brand of justice and he has the money to buy it. And if I know him, which I do, he wants Rachel to pay for shooting his son. Did she really believe that Humphrey was going to beat her to death? I don't know. You're the one with all the answers. Not me." He got to his feet. "This interview is over." With that, Ford Cardwell stomped out.

Chapter Twelve

Ford walked away from his interrogation by the medical examiner feeling angry, scared and confused again. As if he hadn't been all of those since he'd answered his phone and heard a woman screaming. All of this felt…complicated. Complicated like Rachel herself.

Since the phone call, seeing her, overhearing her and Shyla talking earlier, one thing had become clear to him. Love was often blind. His certainly had been. This had made him see Rachel more clearly than he ever had before. The thought almost made him laugh. The shine had definitely come off those old feelings he'd had for her back in college.

Did he have his doubts about her story? Hell, yes. He kept remembering how completely awestruck Humphrey had been with her. Even though Humphrey had known that she'd married him for his money, he'd still loved her passionately, blindly, unconditionally. So what had happened? Whatever it was, it had destroyed not just their marriage, but their lives.

He'd come to the hospital to see Rachel. But after his interview with Hitch, he didn't feel up to it. As he started out of the hospital, though, he received a text from her. Need your help. Rachel. XOXO. Hugs and kisses, followed by a smiley face.

As he pushed open her door, he heard her on the phone. She sounded…happy. The moment she saw him, she quickly disconnected.

"You're in a good mood," he said to her, hating that the medical examiner's suspicions had only made him aware of his own. Her injuries aside, her cheeks were flushed and she was the old Rachel, the one who turned heads when she walked past. It was as if she'd forgotten what had happened not all that long ago, ending with her killing her husband.

"That was my attorney on the phone," she said, smiling. "He said I will be booked tomorrow, but once I'm arraigned, he thinks he can get me bail so I won't have to spend any time in jail. That is such a relief."

"I'm so glad to hear it," Ford said. If her attorney really thought he could get her bail, then he must think the evidence to support her case was sufficient. Did that mean she was innocent? Would a jury see it that way?

"What can I do to help?" Ford asked, noticing that the bruising on her face was more pronounced even though her cuts and abrasions appeared to be healing.

"The sheriff took my clothing as evidence," Rachel said. "I can't show up in court in a hospital gown. I need something to wear."

Ford hadn't thought of that. Of course she would need clothes. He'd been feeling so helpless since he'd arrived here. Now there was actually something he could do to help. "I can buy you whatever you need."

"No, that's really sweet, but I prefer my own clothes

since you can't get anything decent to wear in this town. Would you mind going out to the house?"

This was definitely the old Rachel, he thought, feeling more of the shine come off his infatuation with her. He didn't want to see her house, where she and Humphrey had lived until…it ended.

She gave him a pouty look he remembered so well when she'd wanted something. "It's a terrible inconvenience, I know."

"I don't mind." It felt like the least he could do.

Brightening, she smiled a wide smile, even though it seemed to hurt her to do so. How many times had she turned that smile on him back in college? The medical examiner had asked if Rachel had known how he'd felt about her all those years ago. He looked into her blue eyes. This time when his heart ached, it had nothing to do with an old crush. Of course she knew. Wasn't that why the medical examiner questioned why she'd called him even accidentally?

"I just want to look my best tomorrow in court." The smile instantly disappeared, replaced with tears. "I look awful enough after what Humphrey did to me."

It was so like Rachel to worry about her looks at a time like this. He wanted to laugh at how he'd romanticized coming to her rescue. Had he really thought that her call had been fate? That she'd saved his life? That if anyone could bring him back to life, it would be this woman he'd fantasized about for so long?

"Ford, I don't know what I would have done without you," she was saying. She held his gaze for a long moment before she reached for the pad and pen on the nightstand next to her bed. He wondered why she hadn't asked Shyla to do it for her. Then he felt guilty for even questioning it. Hadn't he told her he would do anything for her?

"I've made a list of what I need from my closet. I put the passcode on there so you can get in."

"That won't be necessary." He turned to see Hitch had come into the room. "I'd be happy to take Ford out to the house to get what you need. They've finished cleaning for your return and I have the passcode to get inside."

"I don't need you to come along," he said quickly. "I can handle it."

"I want to check something out there anyway," the medical examiner said. "We can go now. Unless you have something else you have to do," she said to him.

She knew he had nothing he had to do. "No. Now's fine." He shifted his gaze back to Rachel in time to see dislike written all over her face. Her jaw was tight. Ice glittered in her blue eyes. She quickly changed her expression.

"Perfect," she said and handed him the list before grabbing his hand. Her hand was as cold as her eyes as she smiled up at him and said, "I owe you. Thank you again."

"I'll wait for you in the hallway," Hitch said and left.

Rachel let go of his hand as she stared after the medical examiner. "That woman." She shook her head. "She scares me."

Ford nodded. "She scares everyone."

"No, she has it in for me. I can tell. She's questioned me repeatedly. Is that her job?"

"I think in this instance it is." He wasn't sure if he should tell her Hitch's suspicions. But didn't she have a right to know what she was up against? "From what I hear, she has free rein. The governor apparently asked her to look into your case. At least that's what I overheard when I was down at the sheriff's office."

"Bart's doing, no doubt." Rachel's jaw tightened again, muscles bunching before she unclenched it. "If he gets his way, I'll go to the electric chair."

He could have told her that Montana didn't have an electric chair, but the state still had lethal injection—though it hadn't been used for a while, as far as he knew.

"It's so unfair." She touched the small new bandage on her cheekbone and winced. "It doesn't matter what his son did to me, not just that night but others." She looked away as if embarrassed.

"Why didn't you leave him?" Ford asked impulsively. "If he was hurting you…"

When her blue eyes met his again, they were swimming in tears. "Because I loved him and I thought…" She shook her head. "He was always so sorry afterward and so sweet for a while until…he wasn't." She covered her face with her hands for a moment. "I still can't believe he's dead. All of it just seems like a bad nightmare. I keep waiting to wake up."

"I know." He felt the same way. "I better go. I'll get everything on the list," he said, carefully folding the paper and putting it into his shirt pocket. "I'll bring the clothes back tonight so you'll be ready in the morning."

"I'll never be ready for what I'm going to have to face tomorrow. Why do I have to prove anything? Can't they look at me and see…?" She shook her head. "How could this be happening? I'm the real victim here. Our judicial system is so messed up that a woman can't defend herself against a husband who's trying to kill her?"

He didn't know what to say. "You rest. I'll see you later."

Out in the hallway, Hitch was leaning against the wall, waiting for him.

ON THE DRIVE out to the Collinwood Ranch, Hitch could tell that Ford was still wary of her as if she was the enemy. She'd seen enough from the doorway of Rachel Collinwood's hospital room, though, to see how the woman manipulated him. The question was, how long had she been playing him?

As the huge rambling house came into view, Hitch saw that all the lights in the entire house must be on. She suspected a person could see it from space. The cleaners must have left the lights on. Hitch knew that she hadn't turned them on.

The crime scene tape had been removed since the last time she was out here. The sheriff had told her that he'd hired cleaners with Rachel's permission. Hitch parked and glanced over at Ford. He was staring at the house, looking a little dumbstruck. "Nice digs, huh."

He said nothing as he opened the passenger-side door and stepped out. She followed, curious what he was going to think of this house and the way Rachel and Humphrey had been living.

Once inside the house, she asked, "Would you like to see where it happened?"

"No," he said, glancing toward the kitchen and then looking away as he removed his Stetson.

She saw that he had the list Rachel had given him in his other hand. He seemed to be in a hurry to get this task finished. "You've never been here before?"

His gaze shot back to her. "No. I already told you—"

"It was just a question."

He shook his head. "No question is just a question with you, State Medical Examiner Roberts, and we both know it."

"Please, call me Hitch."

"Are you always so suspicious of people's motives, Hitch?" he asked.

"It comes with the job. Getting to the truth isn't always easy."

"Whom are you kidding?" he said. "You've already made up your mind about this case."

"What makes you think that? Just because I'm suspicious?"

"No," he said with a laugh. "You were suspicious of Rachel right from the very beginning. Admit it."

"Not right from the very beginning."

"Then when?" he demanded.

"If you must know, it was the phone call. I have trouble with coincidences."

"They happen."

She smiled and nodded. "But did it happen this time? The fact that it wasn't just any number she happened to call has to make a person wonder. Calling a man who she knows is still in love with her—"

"I'm not still in love with her."

He sounded adamant about that. "No?" she asked in surprise.

"Can we please get this over with?" he asked, his voice cracking with anger. "You're wrong about me. Humphrey was my friend. If I thought for a minute that she'd somehow set the whole thing up so she could murder him…"

"What would you do, Ford?" Hitch asked. "Walk away?"

"Yes," he said. "And not look back—after I was sure that justice had been done."

She studied him for a long moment. She thought of what she knew about his military career, the man who'd risked his life to save the men on his plane. She believed him. "I suppose we'd better get to that list of yours," she said, turning to lead the way down the hall to Rachel's massive walk-in closet. "I figured you'd need my help to find whatever she's planning to wear tomorrow."

"I think I can manage, thank you."

She laughed. "You haven't seen her closet yet."

As they reached the master bedroom, Hitch walked in and stopped to look back so she didn't miss Ford's reaction. He tried to hide it, but she could tell from his expression that he was taken aback at the size and splendor of the place.

"The closet is this way. They also had separate bathrooms." She walked into the closet with its sitting area. The walls around it were full of clothes, shoes, purses, coats. It looked more like an upscale department store. Hitch wondered if a person could wear all of this apparel even in a year.

"Some people would kill to keep this kind of lifestyle," she said, baiting him in the hopes of getting an honest reaction out of him.

"So Rachel's guilty because she married well?" Ford said.

Hitch turned to look at him, pleased that she'd ruffled his feathers. "She's guilty if she orchestrated what happened here in order to kill her husband for his money. I'm suspicious for the same reasons you are."

"I didn't say I was suspicious." He raked a hand through his thick dark hair. He wore it longer than usual and wasn't used to it, she thought, because this wasn't the first time she'd seen his long fingers raking through it. It certainly wasn't the military cut she'd seen in the photos she'd found of him during his distinguished career.

"You didn't have to say you were suspicious," Hitch said.

He sighed. "What about proof? Don't you need that?"

She met his gaze. "Of course. Proof goes both ways. She could still surprise me. The call could be a coincidence and she could have killed her husband in self-defense." She saw that he hadn't expected that. What she didn't say was that from experience, she knew that Rachel wouldn't surprise her. All her instincts told her that the woman was guilty as hell.

But she could use Ford's help, so she didn't share that detail with him. Rachel trusted him because she believed she could control him. It was Hitch's hope that the woman would lower her guard and make a mistake. Ford was an honorable man. He'd proved that. What would he do if he found out that Rachel had murdered her husband in cold blood? Walk away like he had fifteen years ago? Not until he'd seen justice done, he'd said.

Which was why Hitch was more worried about what Rachel would do if Ford suddenly became more than dispensable. If he became a liability… The thought made her shudder. If Ford found out the truth about Rachel, it could get him killed.

Rachel had no intention of going to prison for the rest of her life. And if Hitch was right, the woman had already killed once. To save herself…? Hitch had no doubt that Rachel would kill again.

"So let me help you with the list." Hitch held out her hand and waited until he handed the note to her. Rachel's handwriting was neat, the list organized right down to the smiley face on the bottom that was for Ford. Just like the small heart the woman had drawn on the smiley face's cheek. And the kisses and hugs. She handed the note back. "Why don't you read it to me and I'll find the clothes?" He seemed relieved to let her. "Let's see, first on the list. Was that a white suit with navy piping?" She moved to the suit area. "Nice that she has everything color coordinated. That will make it easier."

"I'll find the pumps she wants," he said behind her as she thumbed through a variety of white suit sets.

It took them a while, but they found everything on the list. As they loaded the items into the largest piece of luggage from the closet, as per Rachel's instructions on the list, Hitch said, "Tell me about Humphrey. You roomed with him for four years at college, were his best friend. Did you ever see any indication that he would do something like this?"

At first, she didn't think he would answer. But as they carried the luggage out to the car—a large suitcase and Rachel's makeup case—he said, "No, I never did. But that doesn't mean—"

"Did he know how you felt about Rachel?" She sensed the heat of his gaze.

"No. Maybe." He shook his head. "Apparently, I'm pretty transparent—at least according to *you*."

She slid behind the wheel and waited for him to climb into the passenger side. "Why do you think Rachel reached out to you on social media after all this time?"

"She'd heard I was back in Montana. She wanted me to know she was in Montana, too." He looked out his side window for a moment as she started the SUV's engine. Was that when the idea had come to Rachel, the beginning of a plan to kill her husband? "Maybe there was trouble in her marriage and she needed someone she could trust to talk to."

"She doesn't have a friend she could confide in?" Hitch started up the road that would lead them off the ranch. In her rearview mirror, the Collinwood house was dark again—just like the night around them.

"Look, I don't know why she contacted me. Maybe out of nostalgia. Anyway, she has a best friend here. Shyla. Shyla Birch. She's probably the one you should be talking to. She's a friend of Rachel's from college. Shyla should know more about Rachel and Humphrey's marriage than I do."

"Another friend from college?" Hitch said, glancing over at him in surprise. "Did they also only recently reconnect?"

"You make me wish I hadn't said anything."

"You told me because you're worried about Rachel. Like me, you want to know the truth. You're also worried that I might be right."

He shook his head again. "Don't be telling me what I'm thinking, all right?"

"I'm not psychic, but I have good eyesight. Rachel

knew about your accident and discharge from the service, didn't she? She caught you when you were… vulnerable, knowing she could count on you."

His expression said she'd hit the nail on the head.

He glanced away quickly and swore. "I understand you digging into Humphrey's and Rachel's lives, but I really wish you would stay out of mine." His voice was rough with emotion.

"I wish I could, but once you got that phone call? Rachel pulled you right into her mess."

"I don't know how many times I have to say this. She didn't mean to call me. She was probably trying to call 911."

"Glad you brought that up. She botched calling 911, but didn't have any trouble doing it after she killed her husband," she said as she drove away from the Collinwood Ranch.

"He was attacking her during the first call," Ford pointed out.

She glanced over at him. His eyes were dark with anger. Or was it worry? "You're right. It could have been just one of those strange coincidences. Then again, some might even call it fate."

"Not you, though," he said, an edge to his voice. "You only believe what you can prove."

She smiled. "Exactly."

FORD WAS GLAD when the ride out to the Collinwood Ranch was over. After seeing the place, he couldn't help but remember what Shyla had told him about how unhappy Rachel had been living there. It was isolated, but so grand. Rachel had once told him that she wanted one day to live in a palace and have so many clothes to wear that it would be hard to pick out something to wear. And yet she'd been miserable.

He couldn't understand it. Now Rachel was in more trouble than he felt she realized. If Hitch and Bart had their way, Rachel would be going to prison for life or worse. Hitch had done her best to make him doubt what he'd heard. Like her, he had his questions. And maybe, if he was being truthful, his suspicions.

Hitch had dropped him off at the hospital. She'd offered to help him with the luggage but he'd declined. "I can handle it, Ms. Roberts."

"Hitch. I'm sure you can," she'd said before pulling away in her patrol SUV.

"Did you have any trouble finding everything?" Rachel asked anxiously when he brought in her large suitcase and cosmetic bag.

"No. Hitch helped."

"Hitch? You're on a first-name basis with that woman?"

He looked at her, unable to miss the razor-blade sharpness of her tone, and saw that she was visibly upset. "What is it you're asking?"

"She wants to put me in prison. She'll do whatever she can to do that—especially if she thinks she can use you against me," Rachel snapped.

"Because I'm your defense?"

She started to say something, but apparently changed her mind, closing her mouth. Her blue eyes flashed with anger. He watched her try to gain control again. She hadn't expected him to stand up to her.

"I'm sorry," Rachel said quietly. "I know none of this is your fault. It's just that she keeps trying to dig up something against me."

"There's nothing she can dig up, right?" he asked.

"No. But she said she had to go back out to the house. What was that about?"

"I don't know."

"She didn't search the place or act like she was looking for something?"

"No, not that I saw," he said and felt himself frowning. "What would she be looking for?"

"I don't know," Rachel cried and busied herself smoothing the sheets over her. "All of this is so terrifying."

He said nothing, studying her. Even with the years that had passed, he realized with a start that he still knew this woman. While he'd definitely put her up on his own pedestal all those years ago, he didn't think she'd ever truly hidden her flaws from him. He'd just forgotten how she'd used her smile to always keep him on her side when she and Humphrey had an argument.

Ford thought of what Hitch had said, insinuating that he'd put all the blame on Humphrey—rather than Rachel—for forcing him to walk away from the two of them after the wedding.

"I didn't mean to snap at you," Rachel said into the heavy silence that had fallen between them.

"You're under a lot of stress."

"I am," she said, sounding close to tears. "I never thought my life would turn out like this."

"I'm sure Humphrey didn't either." He hadn't meant it the way she'd taken it. Her shocked look, the color that shot to her cheeks, the horrified widening of her eyes, made him regret it.

"You blame me, too?" she said, her voice breaking.

"No, no. That isn't what I meant. I don't know what

happened that day. But I do know that Humphrey would never have wanted it to go so wrong."

She turned her head away, clearly dismissing him.

"I should go," he said and started to move toward the door. "I'll see you in court tomorrow."

As he stepped out of the room, he felt that familiar melancholy take hold of him. He fought to pull himself out of it. He had to see this through. But that thought didn't lift him back up—not the way it had at first.

He considered the woman he'd left in the hospital room as he left. Hitch thought he was a fool. She didn't think he saw through Rachel's helpless act. Rachel was scared, no doubt about that. But the woman had never been helpless. Was that why she'd had a loaded gun? When had she learned to fire it? Or had she just gotten lucky with that one shot?

Ford swore under his breath. Hitch and her suspicions had him doubting everything. Rachel had always used her feminine wiles to get what she wanted. But not all women did. The thought made him think of Hitch.

So what if Rachel loved the finer things in life. That didn't make her a murderer. And Humphrey? Ford couldn't help but remember when they'd been best friends. Like brothers. Had Humphrey turned into a violent man who'd done so much damage to his wife's face and taken a bullet for it?

With a start, Ford realized that if he were a juror at Rachel's trial, he might find her guilty of setting this whole thing up to kill her husband for his money. Never in his life would he have thought Rachel—the woman he'd once adored—could be a cold-blooded killer. Until now. And he hated himself for even considering it.

Chapter Thirteen

The courtroom had a chill to it this morning, Ford thought as he took a seat on the hard wooden bench a few rows back. Bart was already seated in the row behind the prosecutor. Ford watched the two talking quietly. They separated quickly when Rachel was brought in to take her seat alongside her attorney.

Attorney Denton Drake was an elderly man with a pleasant smile and a fatherly attitude toward Rachel, Ford noted. He wondered if the lawyer was good at his job. Rachel needed all the help she could get, if the medical examiner and Bart Collinwood had anything to do with it.

But Rachel was a worthy opponent. In her expensive, beautifully cut white suit, she looked beautiful. Her blond hair was up, gold gleamed at her earlobes and her bandage had been removed. He noted that she hadn't used the makeup he'd brought to the hospital. Her attorney's idea to let the judge see the damage Humphrey had allegedly done? Or had it been Rachel's idea?

Ford saw Hitch drop off some papers for the prosecutor before she spotted him and, to his irritation, slid in beside him.

"Good morning," she said quietly.

"Is it?" He caught her scent, clean and understated, just like the woman herself. He scrutinized her more closely. All the other times he'd seen her, she'd been dressed in either canvas overalls and jacket with *Medical Examiner* stenciled on the back or jeans and a T-shirt with a jean jacket. Her auburn hair was usually pulled up in a knot at the back of her neck. But this morning she wore a nice-fitting gray suit with a white blouse that was opened at the neck. Her hair fell below her shoulders in a cascade of burnished curls. The woman was striking. He wondered how he hadn't noticed it before.

She turned those tropical green eyes on him and seemed to be taking him in with the same kind of scrutiny. He'd had to go shopping for clothes since he'd left in what he'd been wearing, so his jeans and Western shirt were new. His boots were old ones he'd left at his father's place years ago.

"Didn't get much sleep, huh," she said, studying him with that observant look of hers.

Before he could comment, she shifted her gaze to Rachel, who was talking animatedly to her lawyer. "Looks like she got more sleep than either of us."

"The sleep of the innocent," he said.

Hitch chuckled, but then turned serious. "Does that mean you aren't innocent? Or maybe you have more of a conscience?"

Ford shook his head. He wasn't up for another word battle with this woman. He was relieved when the bailiff called out "All rise!" and the judge came into the room. Her Honor signaled for everyone to sit. "Let's make this quick. I have a lot on the docket today."

Ford listened as the charges against Rachel were

read. Deliberate homicide? The judge asked how she pleaded and Rachel said, "Not guilty, Your Honor."

Her attorney asked that she be given bail since this was a justifiable use of force. "She has already surrendered her passport and isn't a flight risk, Your Honor. She has agreed not to leave the state, but simply return to her home north of town."

The prosecutor rose from his chair. "Mrs. Collinwood has sufficient assets to get herself another passport in another name and disappear. I don't think the lack of her passport would stop her."

Rachel's attorney argued that she had no priors, had been a model citizen and that most of the assets were in her husband's name and not accessible to her due to a prenuptial agreement she'd signed. "Mrs. Collinwood is the victim here, Your Honor."

The judge banged her gavel. "Bail is set at five million."

Rachel gasped loudly. In the stunned silence that followed, she turned to look back at Ford, tears in her eyes. He felt that old familiar pull at his heart in spite of everything. But it was accompanied by nausea. He honestly didn't know the truth about her and feared he might never know.

"WHAT WILL HAPPEN to her now?" Ford asked Hitch as Rachel was being led to a jail cell until she could post her bail bond. The courtroom began to fill again. They walked out into the deserted hallway.

"If she can raise enough liquid assets, she'll be released until her trial," Hitch said. "Otherwise, she can post a property bail equivalent to five million dollars."

"If she can't?"

"Then she'll stay in jail until her trial."

"You're that sure this will go to trial?" he asked.

"She killed a man."

"Yes, but—"

"The law doesn't recognize…yes, but."

"What will happen to her if…she's found guilty?"

"During the trial it will be decided if she used justifiable force to stop her husband. If so, she could be charged with mitigated homicide and serve anywhere from two to forty years."

"Forty years!"

"But if the jury finds that she used extreme force that wasn't justifiable, then she could be convicted of deliberate homicide and could be sentenced to life, which is a minimum of thirty years."

He looked sick.

"Or, depending on the judge, she could get ten to a hundred years. We do still have the death penalty in Montana. Lethal injection, though there hasn't been an execution in years."

He clearly couldn't stand the thought. "How is that possible if she was fighting for her life?" Ford said angrily.

"It will be up to a jury and what evidence there is to the contrary."

"Evidence you're gathering against her."

"Only if the evidence is there."

He raked a hand through his hair, looking miserable. "No one is stupid enough to gamble their life for money." She raised an eyebrow, making him furious. "Rachel might be materialistic, but she isn't stupid." He got a smirk at that. "You're wrong. She would have had to know that she might not get away with it."

"Not if she covered all her bets, including making sure you heard enough of the argument that you are now a very large part of her defense. I have to admit, the phone call was pretty brilliant. A medaled war hero just back home? You make a good witness because any jury would see that you're also an honest, honorable man."

He swore under his breath. "You're making Rachel out to be a mastermind criminal and me a saint."

"Most criminals think they're smarter than law enforcement." Her eyes twinkled mischievously. "And I don't think you're a saint. I just think you're a nice guy who fell in love with the wrong woman and has never let himself get over it or the guilt."

"I'm glad you have me all figured out," he said.

She could tell that he was having trouble getting his mind around all this because he didn't think like a criminal. In her job, she'd learned to do just that.

"You still believe she would do this knowing she might go to prison for years?" he said, sounding even more incredulous because he couldn't imagine doing anything like it.

"I'm still on the fence. But it isn't up to me to decide. Once I finish my investigation and provide what evidence I've found to the prosecutor, then it will be up to a jury to make the final decision." She didn't tell him that she'd talked the governor into letting her tap Rachel's phone now that she would be getting out on bail. Hitch couldn't wait to see whom the woman called over the next few days.

"Admit it—you want her to be guilty," Ford said.

"The way you want her to be innocent? No. I just want the truth."

"What makes you think I don't?"

She smiled. "You don't want to believe that she's capable of cold-blooded murder because even if you aren't still in love with her, Humphrey was once your best friend." Hitch started to step away. "Maybe sometime you'll tell me what happened at the wedding. In the meantime, be careful. We have your testimony about the phone call. Your job is done until the trial. Rachel won't be needing you anymore. I don't think you want to stay beyond your welcome or you're going to make her regret calling you."

He shook his head. "You think she used me." Hitch said nothing. "I'm not as blind when it comes to her as you think."

"I hope for your sake that's true, Ford. By the way, someone slid a note under my hotel room door this morning right before I left to come here. You wouldn't know anything about that, would you?"

BACK IN HER ROOM, Hitch considered the note she'd found and bagged as evidence. It was short and to the point: *You need to leave town while you still can.* It had been typewritten, probably on a computer, on plain white paper. She would have it checked for prints, but she wasn't hopeful.

She had ruffled someone's feathers—nothing new there. She didn't think the note was from Rachel, but from someone close to her. Now, who would that be? Not Ford. She'd seen his surprise when she'd asked him about the note.

Spreading out all the evidence she'd collected on her bed back in her hotel room, she went through it again. She was missing something. She could feel it.

But she had someone worried. That gave her hope that she was getting close.

Picking up the photos of Rachel Collinwood's injuries that DCI had sent her, she studied them, wondering what it was that was bothering her besides Ford Cardwell.

He was a principled man who believed in right and wrong. Yet he still had feelings for Rachel Collinwood, no matter what he said. Hitch liked him, which made this case even harder. She hated that he was involved and might get in even deeper before it was over. Would he help Rachel cover up her crime, if she asked? Rachel wouldn't ask unless she was desperate, and that was what worried Hitch maybe the most. What would Rachel do if Ford turned her down?

Hitch tried to concentrate on the cuts, bruises and abrasions on Rachel Collinwood's face in the photos. Frowning, she noticed a distinct mark on the young woman's cheek that she hadn't before. Pulling out her magnifying glass, she took a closer look. It appeared to be an odd-shaped bruise, the kind an unusual ring might make. It definitely wasn't Rachel's husband's ring with the traces of her blood and skin on it.

Pulling out the photos she'd taken during the autopsy, she studied Humphrey Collinwood's ring again. Nothing about it would have made that distinctive bruise. Was there anything in the kitchen that could have made that kind of mark? She studied the photos of the items lying on the kitchen floor and counter. She was becoming more convinced by the moment that the bruise had been made by a ring—just not one worn by the woman's husband.

All along, she'd known that if the murder scene had

been staged, Rachel Collinwood hadn't acted alone. The evidence seemed to be piling up. That was what she loved about criminals. They usually made at least one mistake—often more—even with the best-laid plans. If Hitch could find the person who had been wearing this unusual ring...

Her cell phone rang and she saw that it was the lab on the toxicology samples taken from Humphrey Collinwood. "Tell me you found a drug in his system that would have made him immobile," she said into the phone, knowing it would be the last piece she needed to prove her suspicions were true.

Chapter Fourteen

Ford wasn't sure that Rachel would want to see him. When he'd heard she'd made bail and had been released to return home, he'd called her.

"Ford, I thought you'd gone back to Big Sky," she said, sounding surprised he was still in town and annoyingly reminding him of what Hitch had said. "I appreciate everything you've done for me, but there really isn't anything anyone can do now until the trial. Not that you have to come back for that. I wouldn't want to put you through all of this again. It's bad enough I'm going to have to go through it."

She was dismissing him. Both the sheriff and the medical examiner had his statement. It was all Rachel had needed from him, just as Hitch had said.

"What will you do now?" he asked, hating these gnawing doubts that were haunting him. He knew he'd been listening to Hitch and had bought into her suspicions that he'd been a pawn in Rachel's plan to kill her husband. It wasn't a comfortable place for him—questioning whether the woman he'd once loved hadn't just used him, but instead had set him up so she could get away with the killing of his once best friend.

"There is nothing I can do but hope that all charges

will be dropped and that it won't even go to a trial," Rachel was saying. "The sheriff seems to think I might have a chance of avoiding any more pain." The sheriff might feel that way. But not Hitch. She would keep digging. "Thanks for calling, though," she said, clearly trying to get off the line.

"You'll let me know what happens?"

"Oh, I'm sure you'll read about it in the newspapers."

And just like that, she disconnected. He knew he couldn't leave town feeling like this. He didn't think he could live with these doubts about her. She couldn't have involved him, setting this all up, knowing how he'd felt about her. He wanted to be wrong in the worst way. He had to see her again.

As he topped the rise, he spotted the ranch house sprawled below him in the evening light. He passed a side road that went back into a stand of pines. A stray thought hit him. What a perfect observation point. A person could park in those trees and see all the comings and goings at the main house.

He hated that he'd even thought such a thing as he drove down to the house. Given the way she'd been on the phone, he doubted she'd be happy to see him, but he couldn't leave until he put his mind to rest. This felt unfinished. Not that he knew what kind of closure he expected to get. Certainly not a confession.

A shadow passed quickly before a large plate-glass window as he pulled up in the front yard. Getting out, he walked up the steps to the massive deck that spanned across the front and side of the house. The views from here were incredible—all rolling hills and green pines and pasture all the way to the mountains.

He hadn't noticed when he'd come out here with Hitch. He'd been too uncomfortable in her presence knowing that she was watching him every second.

He paused now, taking it all in, wondering if she appreciated how breathtakingly beautiful it was out here. After ringing the doorbell, he turned again to stare out at the expanse.

Where he lived in Big Sky was different but equally as beautiful. He just hadn't noticed it either since he'd gotten back to Montana. He'd been too much in his own head, too consumed with what had happened when the plane he was piloting went down. Coming here had forced him to feel again, he thought, telling himself he shouldn't have any regrets no matter how this ended.

It took Rachel a while to answer the door. He'd had to ring the bell several more times even though he'd seen her shadow pass that window when he'd driven up. He knew she was home. He'd almost think that she didn't want to see him. Too bad. He wanted to see *her*.

"Ford? What are you doing here?" she said when she opened the door only partway.

"I couldn't leave without telling you goodbye in person."

"Well, isn't that sweet. But you needn't have driven all the way out here." She was standing in the doorway, blocking him as if she didn't want him inside. It made him sad and all the more determined to see what she was hiding.

"I wanted to see for myself how you were doing. I don't like how we left things at the hospital yesterday." She started to say she was fine when he cut her off. "Why don't you invite me in? I promise not to take up too much of your time."

Rachel flushed as if just realizing how rude she was being since he was her alibi—her defense. A fluke, just as he'd thought? Or all part of a murderous plan?

"Of course. I'm sorry," she said, stepping back. "You had sounded on the phone like you were anxious to return home. Come in." She said it loud enough that he felt she was warning someone that they had company. It made him sick inside.

"Are you alone?" he asked, wanting to watch her lie to him.

"Why would you ask that? Of course I am."

He met her gaze, his disappointment in her making him feel even more nauseous. It was true. Over the past fifteen years and probably longer, she'd been the perfect woman in his memory. He'd always imagined her in that dress trying to feed that squirrel. The vision used to make him smile. But apparently the squirrel scene had been a well-planned scheme only to meet Humphrey. Rachel, it seemed, had a talent for staged plots.

"Why don't you come in here?" She motioned toward the kitchen—the same kitchen where she'd shot her husband. "I'll get us something to drink and we can take it out on the deck. It's such a lovely evening." As he followed her into the very white open room, he felt himself cringe. This was where it had happened. Right here. He found himself staring at the floor, imagining Humphrey lying dead there.

"You still like a cold beer, don't you?" she asked, her back to him as she grabbed up some dirty drink glasses and put them in the sink. He'd stopped in the middle of the room and was still staring at the floor, trying not to imagine the gruesome scene.

When she turned, she must have seen his expression. "Are you all right?"

He realized she was standing in front of him holding out a bottle of beer.

"You do still drink beer, don't you?"

He nodded and took it from her. "Rachel, isn't this where—"

Belatedly, she seemed to realize what was wrong with him. She flushed, cheeks hot with anger. "I can't think about that anymore. I have to live here. I can't leave the state. I have to make the best of it," she said, taking her glass of wine and heading for the glass doors. There were two chairs facing the east and a small table between them on the deck. He watched her pick up an ashtray from the table and empty it over the side of the deck railing.

"Are you smoking again?" he asked, feeling shaken by how insensitive she was about all of this.

She shook her head, her back to him. "One of the hired hands stopped by earlier. Nasty habit. Let me get rid of this." She moved past him to return to the kitchen. When she came back out, she had the wine bottle in her hand—a hand she seemed to be fighting to keep from shaking.

He sat down in one of the chairs and watched her slide into the one next to him, exposing a lot of thigh. She wore shorts and a sleeveless top, both in a pale yellow that accented her fresh spray-on tan. There were bruises on her arms that looked like dark fingertips pressed into her flesh. Were they from Humphrey?

"What happened, Rachel?" She looked startled for a moment before he added, "What happened with you and me?"

With a relieved look, she leaned back in her chair and took a sip of her wine.

"Nothing. We've always been good friends. It's my fault I let you walk out of Humphrey's and my life."

"You know I wanted to be more than friends."

She smiled over at him. It wasn't one of her smoldering sunshine smiles.

It held a note of pity that made his heart ache even more. "It was always Humphrey, wasn't it," he said. "From that first day with the squirrel."

"He said it was love at first sight."

"Was that what it was for you?" he asked, suddenly aware of the sweating beer bottle in his hand. He took a drink. It was cold and bubbled all the way down his throat. It was the first sip of alcohol he'd had in a long time.

"I suppose it was love at first sight," she said, not looking at him.

"When did Humphrey...change?"

"Change?" She sounded puzzled by the question as she looked at him and frowned.

Ford met her gaze. "Surely he didn't hurt you at first."

"No, you're right. It started when he was having trouble with his father, the business, you know. He would come home from New York in a bad mood and any little thing would set him off. He knew I wasn't happy here and that upset him. Things just kept getting worse."

"Why weren't you happy here?" he had to ask as he looked out at this beautiful country.

"Are you kidding? After New York City?" She shook

her head. "It's duller than dirt out here. He brought me here to punish me."

"For what?"

She shook her head again and sipped her wine.

He looked away, trying to imagine this Humphrey Collinwood compared to the one he'd lived with most of their time at university. There had never been an easier-going man. "I thought I knew him, so it is so hard for me to understand how this could have happened."

"Why are you questioning me about this? Humphrey had a dark side that he hid from everyone else," she snapped. "It's typical of abusers. I suspect his father abused his mother. That's usually how it works."

"You've researched the subject, have you?"

She didn't answer, but he saw her stiffen in anger. Nor did she look at him. He dragged his gaze away, unable to look at her either.

After a few moments, he relented. "I guess most people hide their...dark sides," he said and finally glanced over at her again. "You're different than I re-member."

Rachel flipped her hair back, her blue eyes spark-ing. "You're angry with me because I had to shoot him." She bit her lip. Tears welled in her eyes. "I'll never forgive myself. Is that what you need to hear? I should never have grabbed that gun. I thought that if he saw it, he wouldn't..." She looked away, wiping at her tears before taking a gulp of her wine.

At that moment, she made him doubt himself. Maybe Humphrey *did* have a dark side. Maybe she *had been* afraid he would kill her. Maybe she *was* here alone. The house was so huge, it probably did take her a while to get to the front door. And the glasses she'd put in the sink? Hadn't she said one of the hired hands had stopped by? It would explain the cigarettes in the ashtray on the deck, as well.

He hated mistrusting her, questioning everything about the young woman she'd been in college, comparing her to the one sitting out here with him right now. The beautiful warm summer Montana evening was like a caress. He realized that, if anything, Rachel had gotten more beautiful. Maybe she was the same young woman he'd known in college. Maybe he was the one who'd changed. Maybe Humphrey had, too. Ford reminded himself that he was a big enough mess without rewriting what had once been the sweetest part of his life, his friendship with Humphrey and Rachel.

And yet he couldn't seem to help himself. "You knew I was half in love with you," he said and met her gaze.

Her expression softened. "I know." She reached for his hand and squeezed it. "I always cared about you, Ford. I wanted the best for you. Humphrey and I never knew why you'd exited our lives like you had right after our wedding. Did you know he tried to reach you numerous times?"

He knew. "You know why I left like I did."

Her light laugh didn't quite come off the way she must have meant it. "You and I should never drink that much together." She turned back to him, something almost coquettish in those blue eyes.

"Neither of us were drunk, Rachel. You dragged me into one of the spare rooms and told me you wanted me to make love to you," he said.

Her lips quirked up on one side. "I believe you kissed me back, and as I remember, that was your hand on my—"

"If someone hadn't tried the door, would you have actually gone through with it?" Would he have? It was something he'd always wondered about even in his guilt over the incident. The memory of it filled him with shame. He'd kissed his best friend's girlfriend and he'd wanted to make love with her. If he could have, he would have stolen her away in a heartbeat. Knowing that, he knew he was no longer Humphrey's best friend and couldn't stand being around the two of them after that.

"We'll never know, will we?" Rachel took a sip of her wine and gazed out at the rolling hills of the ranch.

He put his nearly full beer bottle down on the small table. A breeze blew her long hair into her eyes, and for a moment, she looked like the girl he'd known. "I should go." Getting to his feet, he walked toward the end of the deck that led to where he'd left his SUV. He had no desire to go back through that kitchen.

"Ford!" she called after him.

He turned to look back at her. For a moment, in that soft pale twilight, she looked just as he'd remembered her.

"Thank you."

"I didn't do anything."

"You were here for me when I needed you most. I'll never forget that."

He nodded and started to say it was nice seeing her again. But that would have been a lie. All the pain he'd felt before that phone call seemed like nothing compared to this.

Behind him, he heard Rachel's cell phone ring. Once, twice... She picked up. "Shyla, hi. I'm glad you called." She rose, the chair scraping as she headed back inside the house.

As he passed the front window, out of the corner of his eye, he saw movement. Rachel had lied. She wasn't alone. He wasn't even sure that had been Shyla on the phone.

Chapter Fifteen

"Tell me you found something," Hitch repeated into the phone. If there was a drug in Humphrey Collinwood's system, one that would have made him a walking zombie—

"We ran the entire spectrum of possible drugs," the lab tech said. "I'm sorry. We found nothing."

Nothing? Her mind whirled as she got up to pace her hotel room. She'd been so sure that in order to shoot her husband in the face the way she had, Rachel would have had to subdue him somehow. Otherwise, the reaction of a man who was beating his wife wouldn't have been to just stand there while she pulled a gun. Had he charged her and Rachel got lucky, getting a shot off before he reached her? The marks on his back showed that he'd fallen backward, landing on the broken pottery and glass on the floor.

"Thanks for trying," Hitch said into the phone, hating that she'd wasted the lab's time and her own.

"Wait a minute. Lori's here. She wants to talk to you." She handed over the phone.

"Hitch, I heard about the lab tests you asked to be done. Bradley and I both looked on her computer for anything that might need to be red flagged."

"I'm guessing she was too smart to look up How to Kill Your Husband and Make It Look Like Domestic Abuse."

"No, but something came up that you might find interesting. Mrs. Collinwood did research a common drug used on horses called ketamine."

Hitch sat up, feeling her pulse take off. Bingo. Hitch almost let out a *whoop*, before she caught herself. "But you didn't find it in the drug tests you ran."

"That's because it leaves the system quickly. It works as an anesthesia and is often used on horses. The drug would have been readily available on the ranch. Mrs. Collinwood would have had access to it." Hitch thanked her and quickly got off the phone.

She knew a little about the drug, but quickly looked up the symptoms, especially for large doses. The words leaped out at her.

Blocks sensory perception.
Distortion of environment.
Diminished reflexes.
Muscle rigidity.
Available in a clear liquid or powder form.

"I think I know how she did it," Hitch said to the empty room, unable to hold back her excitement. Unfortunately, it wasn't enough to convict Rachel Collinwood of murder. It was just another piece of a larger puzzle.

Her excitement waned. She had enough to confirm her suspicions—including that odd bruise on Rachel's face. But she didn't have enough for a conviction. Had there been a drug in Humphrey's bloodstream, she could have wrapped up this case. There had to be a way to prove deliberate homicide because all her instincts told her that Rachel Collinwood was lying. She couldn't bear the thought that she hadn't done a good enough job and the woman might get away with murder.

At a sudden pounding at her hotel room door, Hitch quickly opened it. Her mind was already wondering, what now?

"Are you going to let Rachel get away with murdering my son?" Bart Collinwood demanded as he pushed his way into her room.

"I'm still gathering evidence," she said and hurried to gather up the papers and photographs she had strewn across her bed. She finished and turned to look at him. His face was flushed with anger and grief. Her heart went out to him because she felt his frustration only too well.

"I know my son." He shook his head angrily, looking close to tears. "He would never have laid a hand on her unless…"

She felt her pulse jump. "Unless?"

Bart looked away. "He just wouldn't have."

She knew even before she asked the question. "He'd hit her before?"

"No, no," he said at once. "Not my son."

She saw him swallow and knew.

"My wife and I…." He couldn't meet her gaze.

"Your son saw abuse at home is what you're saying."

His head rocked up. "Not like you're thinking. I lost my temper and slapped my wife in front of him once. Humphrey was horrified. He never forgave me or believed it had never happened before or since."

She wasn't sure she believed him. "You're worried he might have done this," she said.

Bart looked ready to deny it with a vengeance. "You

don't know what Rachel is like," he said instead, biting off each word. "She antagonized him, belittled him, did everything in her power to provoke him."

"You're saying she asked for it?" She couldn't keep the edge out of her voice.

"No, that's not what I'm saying," he snapped, looking like a man who wished he'd kept his mouth shut.

"Mr. Collinwood, domestic abuse is often generational."

He let out a curse. "I only lost my temper that one time. I've regretted it ever since."

"It's that attitude—"

"Oh, please. You're just looking for an excuse to let her off. She murdered my son. Humphrey never raised his hand to her. He didn't do this. I'm telling you. I don't know how she pulled it off, but that woman set this whole thing up."

"What if you're wrong and he lost his temper? What if he did do this?"

Bart Collinwood met her gaze and she saw the doubt that she knew had been lurking in there, the fear and guilt. What if he was more like his father than even Bart had realized?

FORD DIDN'T FEEL better as he left the ranch after seeing Rachel. He thought about driving home to Big Sky, but it was dark and late enough that he knew he should wait until morning. Even as he thought it, a part of him wanted to see this all the way through. But rationally, how long was that going to take?

Hitch had her suspicions, but that was about all, from what he could tell. This could go on for weeks or even months before finally going to trial. He got the impression, though, that Hitch wouldn't be on the case that long if she didn't find something fairly soon.

Ford couldn't believe how naive he'd been. He'd thought that by seeing Rachel one last time, he could find some kind of closure. If anything, his visit had made him even more suspicious and upset about the part he'd inadvertently played in all this. Worse, he kept asking himself, "What if Humphrey wasn't an abuser? What if Rachel had lied about everything? Or what if Rachel is telling the truth but goes to prison for thirty years or more for only trying to save herself?"

He honestly didn't know what to believe, except that Rachel had lied to him. His faith in her had been more than tarnished. He'd come here to save her—and had, since his statement about the phone call was on record now. His work here was over. He could get up in the morning and go back to Big Sky. Back to... That was just it. He didn't know what he was going back to.

When he thought about what he'd almost done before her phone call, he felt foolish and embarrassed that he'd let himself fall that low. Maybe it was Humphrey's senseless death and its repercussions, but he knew he'd never try anything that stupid again.

Tonight, though, just the thought of going back to the hotel and packing what little he'd bought since being here was too depressing. He kept thinking about Rachel and the shadow he'd seen at the window. He'd tried to tell himself it had been his imagination. But he knew better. Rachel hadn't been alone. Who was in there with her that she hadn't wanted him to see? The accomplice Hitch suspected had helped Rachel stage the killing?

A set of bright headlights suddenly filled his rearview mirror. He flinched as his gaze went to his side mirror. Only minutes before, there hadn't been another vehicle on this stretch of black two-lane. Not only did the driver have his high beams on, but he was coming up behind him way too fast. The damned fool acted as if he didn't see him. Was the driver drunk?

Ford touched his brakes, but the act seemed to have little effect. He felt his initial alarm grow into fear. The driver wasn't slowing down. He looked to the road ahead. There was no place to turn off the shoulder-less highway. Worse, the highway took a tight turn ahead as it dropped down through the hills and creek bottom.

He didn't realize he'd been holding his breath until the vehicle behind him went flying around him and kept going. His breath came out in a whoosh. He realized that his hands were shaking. He'd been so sure that the driver was going to hit him. Slowing down, he tried to make sense out of the panic he'd felt only moments before. Was this another flashback? No, the driver had wanted him to think he was going to hit him and force him off the road—if not kill them both.

Ford stared after the red taillights. It had been a pickup, but that was all he could be sure of. He hadn't even tried to get the license plate number. Pickups in this part of Montana outnumbered cars and even SUVs. It was probably some ranch hand anxious to get into town to see his girl.

But he knew that wasn't what was bothering him. Had he, for that split second, thought Rachel's accomplice was driving that truck? He had. Because of Hitch's suspicions or his own? He thought about the threatening note she said someone had slipped under her door.

Well, it hadn't been Rachel's accomplice—if there was such a person, he thought with relief.

Until he came around a corner and saw the headlights coming right at him.

Instinctively, he turned the wheel hard to the right and hit his brakes as he went off the road an instant before the other vehicle swept past, only inches from hitting him. He left the pavement, flying off the road and down into the shallow borrow pit.

Something slammed hard against the undercarriage and then he was back up onto the highway before he got his pickup stopped in the darkness. His thundering heart lodged in his throat. He had a death grip on the wheel and was shaking inside.

His gaze quickly went to his rearview mirror, expecting to see the other driver and vehicle crashed in the ditch. But all he saw were taillights before they disappeared over the next rise.

Ford sat for a moment, fighting to catch his breath. The near miss had a tight grip on him, but to his surprise, it didn't call up a flashback. He stared at the empty highway for a moment. His first instinct was to chase down the vehicle. Fortunately, he was thinking clear enough that he didn't. It was long gone. Or maybe it had only gone back to the Collinwood Ranch.

Whoever had come flying around him had been the same pickup that had run him off the road. But did that mean that the person was involved with Rachel? There was only one way to find out.

He did a highway patrol turn in the middle of the empty two-lane and headed back toward the ranch.

Chapter Sixteen

It was getting late. Hitch had been parked in the pines on the mountainside overlooking Rachel Collinwood's house long enough that she'd seen Ford arrive and leave. Soon after that, she'd spotted a pickup kicking up dust on one of the back roads on the other side of the house. Had it come from the ranch house and she'd just missed it? Or had whoever had been driving it parked at a distance and walked up through one of the ravines to the house?

The pickup was so far away and moving at a speed that she doubted she could catch up to it. Had whoever was driving the rig been at Rachel's? If so, the driver had gone to a lot of trouble not to be seen. The accomplice? If so, there probably wouldn't be any more visitors tonight.

She was thinking about leaving her hiding place and going back into town for something to eat when she heard a vehicle approaching. She glanced toward the road into the ranch. No headlights. She watched the dark shape as it headed slowly in her direction. She reached for her weapon.

Setting the loaded Glock next to her right thigh, she waited, curious who was joining her on the side

of the mountain. One of the hired hands? Was this se-
cluded spot with the great view a make-out spot? She
recognized the pickup even before she recognized the
broad shoulders behind the wheel. Ford made several
attempts to get his driver's-side door open and had
to put one of those broad shoulders into it. What was
wrong with his door? she wondered. It was the lawman in her that she noticed such things.

The bigger question was what he was doing here.

As he reached for her passenger-side door, she unlocked it and watched him climb in. "Couldn't sleep?"
she asked.

"Probably for the same reason you couldn't," he
said. She saw that he'd brought his own binoculars.
Had he also brought his own gun? He glanced at hers
lying against her thigh, then turned to look through the
binoculars, glassing the house below them.

"Seems we both had the same idea," she said.

Without looking at her, he said, "Been here long?"

"Long enough," she said and studied him. "How
was your visit with Rachel?" He looked pale even in
the dim starlight and she realized there had to be a reason he'd come back after leaving. "Are you all right?"

"I had a close call on the way into town."

"How close?" she asked, feeling her heart do a little bump.

"Close enough to make me question what's going
on." He sounded as if that was hard to admit.

"What happened?" She thought she might have to
drag it out of him, but he continued after a moment.

"Rachel was acting…oddly. She said she was alone,
but I don't think that was true. After I left, a pickup
came roaring up behind me and then passed me and

kept going over a hundred. I thought it was just some reckless kid until I realized that the driver had gone up the road and turned around and was coming right at me. If I hadn't taken the gully…"

Hitch couldn't speak for a moment. Hadn't she feared something like this might happen? "That's when you sprung your driver's-side door."

"Apparently, since it was fine before that," he said.

"Was it something you said to Rachel?" she asked. "Or something she said?"

He still had the binoculars up, watching the ranch house. "I might have asked too much about Humphrey and the past. Then I saw someone in the house even though she swore she was alone. As I was leaving, she got a phone call. Supposedly it was Shyla, but I'm not sure she was truthful about that either, especially since not too many miles down the road, someone driving a pickup ran me off the road. I know you don't believe in coincidence—"

"That's a lot of coincidences," she said. They were quiet for a long moment. "If Rachel thinks you suspect her and might do anything to recant what you'd heard on the phone…"

"I won't change my story, because it was the truth."

She nodded. "Still, if she thinks you aren't on her side anymore, it could get dangerous." Picking up her binoculars, she studied the house for a moment. Wasn't this what she'd feared might happen? "You need to go back to Big Sky."

He seemed to ignore that. "Is there another way into the ranch besides the main road?"

She lowered the binoculars for a moment to study his face. His binoculars were trained on the house.

"Isn't there always, if you know the ranch well?" she said. "You think he came back here?"

"I didn't pass him on the highway."

"About the truck—I'm assuming you didn't get the license plate number."

He shook his head. "Just a set of bright headlights. But as it went flying by, I caught a glimpse of it. Dark colored. Large pickup. Probably a king cab. That's about it. Except it had a large guard grille on the front of it."

It sounded like the pickup that had been parked outside the morgue. "You didn't see the driver?" He shook his head. She could tell the entire episode—from his visit to Rachel, to him coming up here—had shaken him. He had wanted so desperately to believe in the woman he'd loved. Maybe still loved.

"We're probably wasting our time tonight," Ford said. "If you're right, Rachel planned all this too well. She'll know she's being watched. She's too smart to mess up now."

"Maybe," Hitch said. "But if we're right, her accomplice has already gone off script. Him and his recklessness is her Achilles' heel. I suspect it was his stupid idea to scare you earlier. She won't like it. All he's done is make you more suspicious. She can't have any mistakes at this point. She doesn't need a hothead trying to protect her—but then, that's how he would have gotten involved in the first place. He had to think he was saving her by helping her get rid of her husband. Why not get rid of you, as well?"

He lowered his binoculars to glance at her. "Which means the accomplice isn't as smart or as patient and composed as Rachel," he said.

"He's already made one mistake by running you off the road. I doubt it will be his last. Let's just hope that you're smart enough to get out of town before the next mistake the man makes kills you."

He chuckled at that. "I'm assuming that's the way you dispense advice? Did anyone ever tell you that you're a scary woman?"

She laughed. It felt good to laugh. She'd been worried about Ford because he was so dang trusting and because of how he felt about Rachel. After tonight, maybe his eyes were finally open. Hopefully now he would take her advice and go back to Big Sky, where he should be safe. He was a nice guy. She didn't want to see him hurt any more than he had been.

The dark night, the closeness inside her SUV, the slight summer breeze coming in her cracked open window all made her feel strangely vulnerable, as if she had more in common with this man than she could have ever thought. "You're not the first person to think I'm scary. My ex mentioned it on his way out the door," she said and laughed again. It didn't come off as light as she'd meant it. She could feel his gaze on her.

"I'm sorry."

"Don't be. It was for the best." She glanced at him. "What are you really doing here?"

"Same thing as you. I want to know the truth. I *need* to know the truth since Rachel dragged me into it. Now she wants me gone. I think it's because she's afraid I'm suspicious, and if I think she used me, I might be determined to discover the truth."

"Is she wrong?"

"No," he said.

She stared at Ford. She'd been so sure he was a

sheep and Rachel was a wolf leading him to slaughter. She realized she was going to have to reassess what she thought of him. Love could make you blind and stupid, she knew well. But the smart ones paid attention to the red flags. There were always red flags when a relationship wasn't right.

"So the driver of the pickup," he said, looking through his binoculars again. "I figure he's the boyfriend."

"What makes you think her accomplice is a boyfriend?" she asked, pretending that wasn't exactly her thought.

Ford chuckled. "For the same reason you do. If she orchestrated all of this, then she had to have someone she trusted to pull it off. It had to be someone she had wrapped around her little finger. That usually involves money or sex, in my experience. Sex is the cheapest."

She laughed. "You surprise me," Hitch said, leveling her gaze on him.

"I must look dumber than I am."

She shook her head. "Rachel thinks you're still in love with her and will do anything for her."

He chuckled. "Not after my visit this evening," he said with a grimace. "If she deliberately set Humphrey up to kill him…" Ford looked away for a moment, and she knew he was thinking of the consequences of Rachel's actions if true.

"You know what they say about secrets," Hitch said. "Two people can keep them, as long as one of them is dead. Her accomplice made a mistake tonight by trying to run you off the road. He best watch his back, because I'm betting his days are numbered."

Ford LOWERED THE binoculars and looked at Hitch in the dim light. She had raised her binoculars and was watching the ranch house again. The lights were still on even though it was after midnight. There was a sweet innocence about her face that was at odds with her career choice, he thought, and that determined strength that made her indomitable. "I'm curious. How did you get into this line of work?"

"My dad was a cop. My mother was an attorney. They argued all the time because of their jobs, especially at the dinner table in the evening after work. My brother became a psychologist, my sister a schoolteacher, and I studied to become a medical examiner." She shrugged. "I always liked dissecting frogs in school."

Ford couldn't help but smile. "How does your family feel about it?"

"It makes for interesting discussions on Thanksgiving," she said with a laugh. "What about you?"

"Me?" He shook his head. "Nothing interesting. During my parents' divorce, Dad moved us to Montana. I was just a kid when he and his brothers opened a barbecue restaurant in Big Sky. My uncles, all of them, ended up moving to Montana. My dad's cousin Dana Cardwell Savage lives on a ranch, so I spent a lot of time there growing up."

"You went into the military after college?"

He nodded. "I'd majored in engineering. What I really wanted was to fly."

"And now?"

"Not so much." He picked up his binoculars and scanned the darkness around the house below them on the mountain, desperately wanting to change the subject.

"Have you thought about ranching?" she asked. "It sounds like you enjoyed that."

He hadn't thought about anything. For so long after the crash, the rehabilitation, the end of his military career, he had felt as if he was in a black hole. Rachel had yanked him out of it. He'd always be thankful for that even though he now suspected that she'd had her own reasons for reaching out to him.

Ford thought of Cardwell Ranch and the position his aunt Dana had offered him. He'd thought he'd lost all his enthusiasm for life. He'd been so down, so depressed, so despondent. The doctor's visits didn't seem to be helping the PTSD. But maybe they'd been doing more good than he'd thought.

Because he was beginning to realize that it had been more than Rachel's phone call that had brought him back from the brink. He'd had to hit bottom before he could climb back out. Now here he was.

"I might ranch." Even as he said the words, they surprised him. But he realized they just happened to be true.

HITCH FELL SILENT, aware that something intimate had passed between them. She stared out into the darkness at the house down the mountainside for a few moments.

"You know what bothers me?" Ford asked. "Rachel doesn't seem that heartbroken about Humphrey being dead."

Hitch glanced over at him. "She wouldn't be if she was telling the truth and her husband beat her until she feared for her life and had to protect herself. She also seems to believe that he was having an affair—which he wasn't, according to the woman in question. But the alleged girlfriend did say that Humphrey seemed lonely. He was getting Rachel a horse for her birthday this coming week." She waited for his reaction.

"Doesn't sound like a man who would beat his wife."

Hitch laughed. "The sheriff thinks it made Humphrey look guilty."

Ford lowered the binoculars and looked at her. "He could have been trying to assuage his guilt and make it up to her if he really was abusing her."

"All possible," she agreed as she caught movement out of the corner of her eye and picked up her binoculars again. "Well, how about that? It appears someone is finally making a move."

Hitch pulled out her camera with the telephoto lens and aimed it at the man coming out of the house. Unfortunately, it was too dark to see his face. He'd walked out of the house and was now going around to the back.

She lowered the camera and started the SUV. "I want to see what he's driving." She punched the gas before Ford could move, forcing him to hang on.

"Do you always drive like this?"

"Usually. Am I scaring you?"

"I don't scare that easily," he said, and she sped up.

As they came around the last curve, she spotted the lights of a vehicle racing up the ranch road. "I think I can cut him off down at the highway," she said as she took a side dirt road and increased her speed. He'd asked earlier if there was a back road into the ranch. She'd already checked them all out online, so she had a pretty good idea where the pickup was heading.

They were flying along, bouncing over ruts and

bumps. She glanced over at Ford from the corner of her eye. He looked a little green around the gills. "If you're going to throw up, please do it out the window."

"Throw up?" He scoffed. "I can take whatever you dish out."

She grinned at that. "I do love a challenge."

Not far down the road, she hung a right and came roaring up onto the paved highway before hitting her brakes. Looking both to her right and left, she saw no sign of vehicle lights.

"He could have gone the other way," Ford said just an instant before a set of headlights topped a rise and shot toward them.

"Let's see if we can get a make and model of this car," she said as she pulled to the edge of the road and cut her engine and lights. "A license plate would be even better."

A dark-colored pickup sped past at the same time Hitch restarted the SUV and gunned the engine. Her vehicle jumped up onto the highway again, tires squealing as she went after the truck.

FORD FOUGHT BACK the nausea. He would rather die than prove Hitch right by vomiting. His stomach roiled, though. The wild ride was giving him flashbacks of his plane crash—as well as his recent race to the end of a cliff. He felt disoriented and out of control. Sweat broke out on his back as he struggled to separate the events and fight off the anxiety attack.

Taking deep breaths, he stared straight ahead at the two red taillights. The lights grew larger and larger as Hitch closed the distance. He saw that the back of the pickup was covered in mud, making it almost impossible to read the license plate.

"It's a Chevy half-ton pickup. Newer model. Dark blue or gray. Hard to tell with all the dust on it," Ford said, concentrating on the truck rather than the flashbacks that flickered like an old-timey movie in his head. He could smell the smoke, feel the flames licking at him as he fought to get his men out before the plane's gas tank blew.

"Can you read the plates?" Hitch asked.

"Starts with 40."

"Big Timber."

"I think it's 19 after that, but I can't read the rest," he said.

She turned on her blinker and passed the truck, getting the SUV up to over a hundred. "You might want to duck down. If he sees you and recognizes you—"

"I'll take my chances, thanks." His head hurt and he still felt sick to his stomach. Given the vibration of the SUV, he estimated that she had to be pushing the SUV to over a hundred and thirty. They zoomed past the pickup.

"Well?" she asked as she whipped back into the right lane and kept going.

"He was wearing a cowboy hat, so I couldn't see much of his face." She shot him a look, making him more nervous. "The road," he said. "Also, aren't there deer out here at night?"

"Was the man behind the wheel the one who had tried to run you off the road earlier?"

He shook his head. Wrong pickup, he was pretty sure. His head ached. He could hardly think. But he was sure this wasn't the same driver or the same pickup.

"Well?" she asked.

He rubbed his temples. "I don't think so, but honestly, I don't know." He felt as if he had disappointed her.

"We should go back and get your rig," Hitch said, hitting her brakes and doing a highway patrol turn in the middle of the road. Once they were headed in the opposite direction again and slowed down, she said, "Tell me you can do better than that on a description of the man since you're about to get another look at him."

He looked out the windshield as the pickup sped past. "Strong jaw, straight nose. Dark designer stubble. Nice looking. Are we assuming this is the boyfriend? The age looks about right. Maybe a little young for her."

She chuckled at that. "I guess I'll find out once I know who he is."

Chapter Seventeen

It didn't take long for Hitch to match the make and model of the vehicle the man had been driving last night to the partial plate number.

"Who is Lloyd Townsend?" she asked the sheriff when she walked into his office first thing the next morning.

Charley didn't look happy to see her. "Why are you asking about Lloyd?" She waited him out until he finally sighed and said, "He's one of our most respected businessmen in town. You don't want to go messing with Lloyd. Everyone in this town loves him. He's always the first to donate to any cause. Salt of the earth."

"Got it," Hitch said and turned to walk out.

"Hold up there a minute," the sheriff said. "Mr. Collinwood is on my back about his boy's body being released."

"He can take him today," Hitch said and saw Charley's surprise. "I think I have everything I need."

"To convict that poor woman?" the sheriff demanded, an angry edge to his voice.

"If she's guilty, then hopefully yes," Hitch said and left the sheriff's department. As she headed out the front door, she spotted Ford leaning against his pickup as if waiting for someone. She smiled, realizing she was that someone.

"HAVE YOU HAD BREAKFAST?" Ford asked as he pushed off the side of the vehicle and stepped toward her.

"As a matter of fact, I haven't."

"Well, I'm hungry and I don't like to eat alone. Hop in. I'll drive."

He drove the few blocks to the café, neither of them saying anything. Once inside, they sat across from each other in a booth.

"Why do I suspect you have something on your mind besides breakfast?"

He nodded. "I had a lot of time to think last night. I'm not as convinced that Rachel had something to do with me being run off the road." Hitch nodded as if she wasn't surprised. "Did you find the man we saw last night coming out of her house?"

"Might have." She pulled out her phone, tapped in the name and came up with a photo of an elderly man with a thick head of gray hair. "How old would you guess the man was who you saw driving the pickup?"

"Forties maybe. He could have been younger. As you know, I didn't get a good look at him either time."

She turned her phone screen so he could see it. "Could he have been sixty-seven with gray hair and glasses?"

Ford chuckled. "My eyesight is better than that. Who's the man?"

"Lloyd Townsend," she said, putting her phone away. "Clearly not the one driving last night. But it was his truck." The waitress brought them coffee, water and menus, and they both ordered quickly without hardly glancing at their menus.

Ford's mind was on the woman across the table and their surveillance adventure last night. He'd seen another side of Henrietta Roberts, one he rather liked. "I don't think that pickup and driver was the same one that ran me off the road. The more I've thought about it, I think it was just a drunk driver and I was being paranoid."

"That it was a coincidence that this driver showed up shortly after you left Rachel Collinwood's house? Like the coincidence of her pocket dialing you just before she killed her husband?"

He met her gaze. "What if you're wrong about her? What if we both are?"

Hitch leaned her elbows on the table, giving his question some thought. "Then the lack of evidence will allow her to either walk or get a lighter sentence. She did kill a man. If she truly was an abused wife, she needed to leave him—or in this instance do what she could to get away from him. If she'd hit him with a frying pan, well, she would have had a better chance of getting off. Having the gun makes it look as if she was laying for him."

"What if she was afraid to leave Humphrey?" he asked. "I've looked into this a little, and from what I've read, the highest risk time for a homicide is not when she's *in* the relationship but when she's trying to leave it."

"In order to prove self-defense, she has to prove that she was or at least believed that she was in imminent danger. The problem is that she had the gun. Did she have other alternatives other than to use what could be seen as unreasonable force? That will be up to a jury to decide. Why did she have the loaded gun handy? If she feared they were going to have a knock-down, drag-out fight, why wouldn't she get out of there?"

"Because she felt safe. She had the gun if things got out of control," Ford said. "If he'd beaten her up before, then this time she planned to stop him."

"We can't know what was going through her mind at the moment she pulled the trigger. We might never know."

The waitress brought their breakfast orders and they ate in a companionable silence, until Hitch pushed her plate away and asked, "What do you know about Humphrey's parents? Did he ever mention that they didn't get along?"

"You're asking if Bart was abusive." He frowned. "You found out something about Humphrey." He could tell that she didn't want to share the information with him.

"Bart let it slip that his son had seen him hit his wife. A slap. Bart swore it was the only time and that Humphrey had been horrified and never forgave him."

Ford groaned as he raked a hand through his hair. "You're thinking father like son."

"It could be that Humphrey mentioned what he'd seen to Rachel. It could have given her the idea. Or he could have been so angry with her…"

"This makes you have doubts," he said, shaking his head. "So your mind isn't completely made up after all." He smiled at her, liking her even more. Not that he wanted it to be true of Humphrey.

She looked at the time on her phone. "I have to go. Thanks for breakfast."

"My pleasure." He watched her leave, wondering how Lloyd Townsend's pickup played into all this.

LLOYD TOWNSEND OWNED a hobby ranch on the Yellowstone River just a few miles from town. As Hitch drove up into the ranch yard, she spotted the pickup she'd seen last night and parked beside it.

Getting out, she walked over to the truck and looked inside, seeing nothing of interest.

"Can I help you?" asked a male voice from the front porch of the house. She hadn't heard anyone come out.

Turning, she considered the elderly man for a moment, before she stepped to the house, stopping at the bottom of the stairs. "I'm Hitch Roberts, state medical examiner." He seemed to be waiting for more. "I'm currently working on a local case. Were you driving this pickup last night sometime after midnight?" She waited, wondering what his answer would be. If he lied, he might be involved. If he didn't—

"No," he said, frowning. "You're sure it was my truck? After midnight?"

She nodded. "It was this truck. Who else might have been driving it?"

Lloyd Townsend rubbed his jaw for a moment before he said, "I suppose one of my sons could have taken it. What's this about?"

"I was hoping the driver of your pickup last night might be able to help me with the case I'm working on. Are your sons around?"

"I believe they're out by the corral behind the house working with one of the horses. You're welcome to go back there. It's just around the side of the house." He made a motion with his right hand and started to turn back inside.

The light caught on his hand from the movement.

"Excuse me—I just noticed your ring," she said as she climbed a couple of steps to take a closer look. Lloyd looked down at his ring and smiled as he held out his hand so she could admire it. "It's quite unusual."

"It's our family crest," he said with no small amount of pride. "Both of my sons wear one. Rather a family tradition. Are you familiar with the history of the coat of arms?"

"I can't say I am," she said, her pulse having jumped when he'd told her that both of his sons also wore the same design of ring.

"Coats of arms were used for centuries to identify a certain family. They were created for the battlefield," he said, clearly warming to the subject. "Other knights couldn't tell who was inside of a suit of armor, so they created symbols to attach to the armor. Not to be confused with the crest, which is only a portion of the coat of arms that was worn above the helmet."

"Fascinating," she said, taking the steps back down the stairs. "Thank you for the information. Oh, by the way, what are your sons' names…?" As she went around the side of the house, she called the sheriff on her phone. "Meet me at Lloyd Townsend's ranch as quickly as you can." She hung up before he could argue. She figured he'd come racing out here, hoping she hadn't upset a town favorite.

As she reached the corner of the outside of the house, she spotted the corral. One of the sons was leaning on the corral fence, while the other was inside it with a large bay he was apparently trying to break.

As she joined the one outside the corral, she climbed up on the fence to watch. It was a beautiful bay being green broke by what appeared to be the youngest son, Paul. Out of the corner of her eye, she saw the cowboy next to her look over.

"You must be John," she said, turning toward him. His father had described him as the oldest and bigger of the two. "I'm Hitch. Hitch Roberts, state medical examiner." She held out her hand, he shook it and she went back to watching what was going on in the corral, even though her mind was on the ring on his right hand. "He seems to know what he's doing."

She was wondering if she could get any of Rachel Collinwood's DNA off it after all this time. The lab wouldn't need much, and with the deep grooves of the ring…

"Paul *should* know what he's doing. He's been at this most of his life. Not that he won't hit the dirt before the day is out," John said with a laugh.

What their father hadn't told her was that Paul was the more handsome of the two. In fact, he was gorgeous, from his muscled lean body to his chisel-cut jawline and the styled stubble covering it. With his hat on, he definitely appeared to be the man behind the wheel of the pickup last night. She could also see how he might turn the head of a married woman—and vice versa.

"You here about a horse?" John Townsend asked.

"Actually, I'm looking for whoever was driving your father's pickup last night north of town sometime after midnight," she said.

"Don't look at me," John said. "I was in bed by then."

She noticed the wedding band on his left hand. Married. So he'd have an alibi—if he were telling the truth. "Anyone else drive the truck besides you, your father and your brother, Paul?"

"Not that I know of."

"Well, that narrows it down, doesn't it," she said and watched as Paul finished putting the saddle on the bay. He led the horse around the corral a few times before he swung up into the saddle. His behind hadn't touched leather but for a moment before the bay began to buck.

Hitch and John jumped back as the horse tried to knock Paul off by putting him into the corral fence. To his credit, the cowboy hung on longer than she suspected most would have before he and the horse parted ways.

Paul was getting up from the ground and dusting himself off when the sheriff arrived. Hitch went to meet him away from the corral and the two Townsend sons. She could tell Charley was already upset from her call. He was about to get even more upset, she thought. "I need the rings both of the Townsend sons are wearing."

"What the hell?"

"One of them—I suspect the youngest, Paul—paid a visit to Mrs. Collinwood late last night."

The sheriff looked both surprised and confused. "Maybe he was just—"

"Giving her his condolences?" she asked.

Charley spurted for a moment before he demanded, "Why in the hell do you want their rings?"

"For evidence."

"Evidence of *what*?"

"Murder. You do realize, Sheriff, that this is what the case is about, don't you? Finding out what really happened at the Collinwood Ranch and why Humphrey is dead."

He stared at her, openmouthed. "What are you talking about? You think one of the Townsends—"

"I want to bring Paul in for questioning. The governor has given me the authority to do whatever I have to. But you know them, so I'd prefer you do the honors."

The sheriff let out an angry sigh and stared at his boots for a moment. "If you're wrong about this—"

"I'll take full responsibility."

RACHEL STOOD IN the middle of the kitchen trying to catch her breath. She'd never had an anxiety attack, but she thought this must be what one felt like as she tried to calm herself.

She hadn't recognized the number when she'd gotten the call. For a moment, she'd almost not taken it. "Hello?"

The moment she'd heard the voice, she'd snapped, "Shyla, why are you calling me from some number I don't recognize? I almost didn't pick up."

"I borrowed a phone. I'm at the sheriff's department. I just heard the craziest thing. That medical examiner? She and the sheriff just went out to the Townsend place and confiscated both Paul's and John's rings. Supposedly it has something to do with Humphrey's death."

That was when all the air in the kitchen felt as if it had been sucked out. She'd had to grab the counter to steady herself. "Why would she care about their rings?"

"Beats me. Apparently," she said, lowering her voice, "they're evidence. But evidence of what? Not only that the medical examiner knows that one of the Townsends came out to your place last night. You aren't still—"

"Of course not." She tried to catch her breath. "I thought I heard someone. I was in the tub. Why would he come out here?"

"Why do you think? What if he tells them about the two of you…?"

She groaned inwardly, still fighting the lack of oxygen. She felt as if a ton of bricks had fallen on her chest.

"Well, I thought I'd warn you," Shyla said. "Listen, it sounds like the medical examiner is building a case against you."

"I know. But she's wasting her time. There isn't anything to find."

"Are you sure about that? Rick thinks it isn't just the medical examiner but Ford who's the problem. Did you and Ford have an argument?"

Rachel had to sit down and put her head between her knees. "Tell Rick that everything is fine and for him not to worry about me. You either. I have to go."

Chapter Eighteen

Paul Townsend looked more amused than anything as he lounged in one of the chairs across from the sheriff's desk.

"The medical examiner wants to ask you a few questions," Charley said, sounding apologetic as he leaned back in his chair and made it perfectly clear that none of this was his idea. "I'm sure it won't take long."

Hitch tried not to grind her teeth. She'd worked with enough small-town sheriffs that this shouldn't come as a surprise. "I happened to see your pickup on the road north last night after midnight. Want to tell me where you were coming from?"

The cowboy seemed to lose some of his cockiness for a moment. "Just went for a ride."

"A ride? No place in particular?"

"Nope."

"Paul, I should advise you that I witnessed you leaving Rachel Collinwood's house not long after midnight. I took photos of you and then later of the pickup you were driving."

He sat up a little and shot an uncomfortable glance at the sheriff as if he expected Charley to bail him out.

Hitch gave the sheriff a warning look, daring him to do so. "So what? I wanted to see how she was doing."

"At midnight? That's when you decided to stop by?"

Paul looked around the office for a moment. "What's this about?" He wasn't as cocky as he'd been earlier.

"How did you get the scrapes on your knuckles?" Hitch asked.

He glanced down at his hands as if surprised to see them. "I don't know. Working on the ranch. You saw me working today. I get beat up." He sounded proud of that.

"What is your relationship with Mrs. Collinwood?" Hitch asked.

His eyes widened. "We don't have a relationship exactly."

Hitch leaned toward him. "I know you didn't pull the trigger, but how were you involved in Humphrey Collinwood's murder? If you tell the truth—"

"Wait! What? I don't know what you're talking about," he said, shooting to his feet.

"I'm talking about you doing less time in prison by telling us what really happened out at the ranch the day Humphrey Collinwood died. Otherwise, you will go down with her."

"No, you got it all wrong. Yes, I went out there last night. I don't know what I was thinking. I just wanted to see if she was all right." Hitch cocked her head at him and waited. He hung his head. "I'd had something to drink, okay? Maybe too much. I got to thinking about her."

"How long have the two of you been having an affair?" she asked.

He wagged his head. "It isn't like that," he said as

he sat back down looking deflated. "It was just a few times."

"When was this?" Hitch asked.

"A year or so ago. I tried to see her again, but she…"

"Was married."

"Yeah," Paul said, lifting his head. "Look, my father doesn't know." He glanced at the sheriff. "Does he have to find out?"

"When was the last time you saw her before last night?" Hitch asked.

"A year ago. I called a few times, and when she quit taking my calls, I gave up. But I swear, I just went out there to make sure she was all right, but she didn't answer the door, so I left."

"I saw you coming out of the house," Hitch said.

He nodded. "I know the passcode. Like I said, I was worried about her, so I went inside, but her bedroom door was closed. I knocked on it, thought I heard water running. I got to thinking that she might shoot me, too—you know, thinking I was a burglar or something—so I left."

"When you were involved with Rachel Collinwood a year ago, did you notice any bruises on her that might have indicated she was being abused?"

He shook his head. "But I could tell she was afraid he would find out, you know?"

Hitch thought she did. "Would you please remove your ring, Mr. Townsend?"

He closed his hand into a fist. "Why?"

"I'd like to take it for evidence," Hitch said.

Paul looked at the sheriff, then back at her. "You can't take my stuff without a warrant, right?" he asked, his gaze back on the sheriff.

"If you are unwilling to relinquish it and allow me to take it as possible evidence, then I will have to ask the sheriff here to arrest you for conspiracy to commit murder, at which time your possessions, including your ring, will be taken and used as possible evidence in the case."

"But I just told you—" The cowboy looked like a trapped animal. "I want a lawyer."

She looked to the sheriff. "Would you please arrest Mr. Townsend for me, Sheriff?" Her look said, *Don't make me call the governor.*

"I'm sorry as hell about this, Paul," Charley said, lumbering to his feet. "Why don't you just give her the damned ring?" The cowboy covered the ring with his other hand and shook his head. "She's going to get it, one way or another," Charley continued. "You want to spend time behind bars over a stupid ring? Don't make me have to arrest you."

Paul angrily jerked off the ring, rose and threw it down on the sheriff's desk. As Charley reached for it, Hitch beat him to it, using her shirtsleeve to pick it up before bagging it.

"I want that ring back," Paul said angrily. "And a public apology."

The sheriff sighed deeply before saying, "You're free to go now and we'll make sure at some point that you get your ring back."

"But let me know if you decide to leave town," Hitch called after him as the cowboy stormed out and got on his cell phone. "I wonder who he's calling. Rachel Collinwood to warn her?"

"He's probably just callin' for a ride back to the ranch," Charley said, picking up his keys. "You might recall that he rode with me." The sheriff shot her an incredulous look as he walked out after Paul.

"I'm going to need his phone records," Hitch said to his retreating back.

She was anxious to check the ring against the photographs of Rachel's bruises before sending it to the lab. Back in her hotel room, she pulled out her magnifying glass. She studied first the bruise, then the surface of the ring. Tilting the ring this way and that, she imagined slipping it on her finger.

"If I were to punch someone…" She made the motion with the ring still in the evidence bag and then checked the position of the ring against that of the bruise. The resemblance was there. But would a jury see it? Maybe.

Her real hope, she knew, was what the lab would find. The grooves in the ring's design were so deep… She had to believe that the evidence would still be there. Unless Paul Townsend was telling the truth.

"I KNOW. I UNDERSTAND. No, I—" The sheriff pulled the phone away from his ear for a moment. "Lloyd, I totally agree with you. But it's out of my hands. This came all the way down from the governor. I can't do anything with that woman." He listened to the man rant and rave and threaten to sue. "I don't know why she wanted your sons' rings. I know they're valuable. Nothing's going to happen to them. But at least Paul's not behind bars. Be happy about that. If she'd had her way…" He pulled the phone away again and looked up to find Ford Cardwell standing in his doorway. "Lloyd, I have to go. Do whatever it is you have to do." He hung up. "What do you want?" he snapped and then quickly apologized. "Sorry, it's been one of those days."

"I didn't mean to interrupt," Ford said.

"No, actually, I should thank you. What can I do for you?"

"I was looking for Hitch," Ford said.

Charley made a rude sound that went with the face he pulled. "Well, she isn't here. She was. I have no idea where she is. Probably starting trouble somewhere else. She won't rest until she has this whole town up in arms." He realized Ford was still standing there. "Try the morgue. I know it's late, but that's where she's been hanging out. You know where that is?" He didn't wait for an answer and quickly gave him directions. Big Timber was small enough that it was pretty easy to get around.

As Ford started to leave, the sheriff took his first good look at the man since he'd appeared in the doorway. "You don't look good," Charley said and frowned. "You look like someone punched you in the gut. You all right?"

"I've been better."

"You sticking around?"

"I'm not sure."

Charley nodded. "But you'll be back for the trial—if it comes to that. Rachel's going to need your testimony, so you'd best take care of yourself. Without you…"

Yes, without him, Rachel wouldn't have as strong a case. "Thanks again for the directions." As he left, the sheriff's phone rang. He heard him curse and say, "Who wants to chew off my ear now? On top of everything, I'm missing my supper, damn it."

So MUCH HAD happened in the past seventy-two hours.
Hitch had gone through all her notes again. She'd stuck
her neck out bringing Paul Townsend in. There was
pressure on the governor from both Bart Collinwood
and Lloyd Townsend now. She had to wind things up
and soon.

After pacing her hotel room floor, she knew there
was only one way she could unwind. Drive. As she
walked out of the hotel, she noticed something flap-
ping in the breeze on her windshield. A piece of folded
paper under the wiper of her SUV. She pulled on the
extra pair of latex gloves she always kept in a pocket
when on a case and carefully removed the typed note.

The message was much like the other one that had
been slipped under her hotel room door.

You messed with the wrong people bitch.
Leave town or wish you had.

She bagged the note—just as she had the first one—
shaking her head in wonder. It wasn't the first time
she'd received threatening notes in her career. Nor did
she suspect it would be the last. Such notes never made
her want to leave town. On the contrary, it assured her
that she was on the right track—and getting too close
to the truth for someone's comfort.

Like the first note, this one had been written probably on a computer on plain white paper. She doubted it
would have any fingerprints on it either, but she would
have the lab check.

She'd been planning to go for a drive. It helped her
to think. But the note had changed her mind. She decided that the walk to the morgue might be a better
choice. Her assumption was that the note had been
from Rachel's accomplice. But it could have just as

easily been from someone in the Townsend family. Or even someone who believed Rachel was being treated unfairly. Her friend from college?

The walk to the morgue wasn't far, but it was off the main drag. The streets here lacked sidewalks, pavement and lighting. She walked along the edge of the packed dirt road, thinking about Paul Townsend. He was young and handsome and naive enough that he could have fallen for not just Rachel Collinwood but her alleged need to protect herself from her abusive husband. Paul could have thought he was saving her, being her hero, seeing the killing of Humphrey Collinwood as ridding the world of a monster.

Lost in thought, she didn't hear the vehicle coming up behind her until the sound of the engine roared. Hitch only had enough time to glance over her shoulder to confirm what she already knew. The driver was bearing down on her.

Chapter Nineteen

Hitch wasn't at the morgue. Nor was she in her room when he called the hotel. Ford thought about what the sheriff had said about him taking care of himself. He couldn't remember the last time he'd eaten more than a few bites of anything.

As he drove through Big Timber, he looked for a place to eat. There weren't that many options this time of the night. He'd gone down a side street when he spotted red taillights disappearing in the distance. Closer, a person came stumbling out of a hedge along the road directly in front of him. He threw on his brakes. With a shock of recognition, he saw that it was Hitch and that she was injured.

BLINDED BY THE HEADLIGHTS, Hitch jerked away from the man who ran toward her, thinking it was the same one who'd tried to run her down.

"Hitch, it's me." She felt a wave of relief as she recognized Ford's voice. She let him take her in his arms, because right now she wasn't steady on her feet. The pickup that had tried to run her down had come too close. She'd felt the brush of the bumper against the side of her thigh. She didn't think anything was broken from the contact or her dive into the hedge, but she hurt all over and was definitely shaken.

Whoever had been driving that truck hadn't just been trying to scare her. If she hadn't thrown herself into the hedge, the impact would have killed her.

"What happened?" He sounded scared. "That pickup that just went past? Did it hit you?"

"No. I'm all right." But her legs seemed to give out under her because of the shock that came with the re-alization of how close a call it had been. "I just need to sit down for a minute."

He caught her, scooping her up, her trembling in his arms as he carried her over to his truck. Reaching behind her, he opened the door and set her down on the seat. "I'll take you to the hospital."

"No hospital," she said quickly. "I'm not hurt. Just shaken up."

"Your cheek is bleeding."

She leaned back, eyes closed, until the dizziness passed as she tried to catch her breath and calm down. When she opened her eyes, she saw that he'd already dug out a first-aid kit. She smiled up into his hand-some face, wondering where he'd been her whole life.

"This is going to hurt," he said as he wiped away the blood with an alcohol swab. She winced more from the cold liquid than the pain. "Sorry," he said, his fingers so gentle that she felt her eyes smart. She wasn't used to a man treating her as if she were made of glass. She was too independent, too strong, too determined. At least that was what most men she'd dated had said.

But not this man, she thought as she watched him open a sterile bandage and apply it to her cheek. "Thank you." Her voice came out a hoarse whisper, almost choked with an emotion that surprised her. She told herself it was just her brush with death and his gentle kindness. But as he finished bandaging her cut and looked down into her eyes, she felt a jolt clear to her core. Then his fingers were cupping her uninjured cheek. His rough thumb pad slipped under her chin to lift it as he leaned down and kissed her. The impulsiveness of the kiss, the surprise of it, the tenderness of it all caught her completely off guard.

His lips brushed hers, urging them open. They didn't put up much of a fight. As her lips parted, he cupped the back of her head, deepening the kiss. She grabbed a handful of his shirt, drawing him even closer as she lost herself in the startling passion of their combined kiss.

A groan rose from deep in his chest as he drew back a little to look into her eyes again. "I'm sorry. Here you are injured, and I…" His warm, strong fingers still holding the back of her head were buried in her hair. He seemed as shocked by the powerful kiss as she was.

Still bunching his shirt in her fists, she pulled him down for another kiss. He dropped his mouth to hers and deepened the kiss, this one even hotter than the first.

She loosened her hold on his shirt. His look mirrored hers. Wow. Everything about the kisses had been unexpected in so many ways.

"I've been wanting to do that for a very long time," he said, his voice sounding rough with emotion as he drew his hand from behind her head and straightened. "The timing, however—"

"Was perfect. I hadn't realized how much I needed that." She smiled at him and he smiled almost shyly back. "You don't find me too scary, then?"

"Oh, I wouldn't say that." He chuckled as he tucked her into the seat and closed the passenger-side door. She watched him walk around to the driver's side and slide behind the wheel.

"Any chance the truck driver just didn't see you?" he asked.

"No. Whoever was driving that truck wanted me dead," she said, leaning her head back against the seat and looking out into the darkness, thinking not about her near-death experience, but Ford and that kiss.

For a moment, he simply sat behind the wheel before he glanced over at her, drawing her attention back. "You feel better?" She could only nod. "You're probably not hungry."

"Starved," she said. Her stomach rumbled at the thought, reminding her she hadn't eaten all day.

He chuckled and started the engine. "Any chance you got the license plate on the rig that almost hit you?" he asked as he drove them to the local burger shop.

She thought of that glimpse she'd gotten before the headlights had blinded her. She could almost hear the roar of the engine as the driver bore down on her. "It happened too fast. Too dark to even make out a model of the pickup. All I really saw was the metal guard on the front. I think I would recognize it, if I saw it again."

"I think I know that grille guard," Ford said. "I didn't mention it because most trucks around here have the guards on them because of all the deer on the highway at night. But the truck that ran me off the road had a huge shiny metal guard on the front, as well. I think we're looking for the same man."

"If I were a betting woman, I'd say he's the same man Rachel Collinwood talked into helping her kill her husband."

IT FELT IRONIC, Ford thought as he and Hitch finished their cheeseburgers, fries and chocolate milkshakes and he drove her back to the hotel where they were both staying. He'd come here for Rachel. He would leave here missing Hitch. In a few days' time, he'd come to admire this strong, capable woman.

He scoffed, knowing it was more than that or he wouldn't have kissed her. He felt a fire again in his belly that he'd thought had been extinguished. Desire. He'd actually forgotten what that felt like. But Hitch had fanned the flames and now he burned inside for her and the passion he'd felt kissing her.

All during the meal, Hitch had seemed her old self—except for the bandage on her cheek and a few scratches and probably bruises from her dive into the bushes. They'd talked about growing up in Montana—skirting away from the investigation. It had been one of the most pleasant meals he'd had in a long time.

When he'd walked her to her door at the hotel, there'd been a moment when they'd both seemed to hesitate.

"Good night," he said and took a step back. As badly as he would have loved to be invited into her hotel room, he knew it was too soon. "I'm right down the hall, if you need me."

She'd nodded and smiled. "I'll keep that in mind."

His cell phone rang right after he'd stepped inside his hotel room. For a moment, he was hoping it was Hitch. She'd been just as surprised by what they'd shared. He'd seen it in her eyes, in the trembling of her lips. She wasn't one to leap blindly. At least not when it came to men. He wasn't sure how he knew that, just that he did.

Still, he tried to hide his disappointment. "Dad, I was going to call you. I'm coming home tomorrow."

"Good. You sound...good."

Ford had to smile. He and his father were both short on words in uncharted territory. He knew Jackson had been worried about him. Hell, Ford had been worried about himself.

"Coming over here has been good for me," he told his father.

"Did you resolve anything with Rachel?" Jackson asked.

He chuckled. "Did I get closure? Yeah, I did. I feel better about a lot of things." He envisioned Hitch for a moment.

"I can't tell you how glad I am to hear that," his father said. "It will be great to have you back."

As he disconnected, he saw movement on the street below the window and looked out. Hitch? It was just like her to go back out to the Collinwood Ranch tonight to see if she could catch the man she suspected of being the accomplice visiting Rachel again.

He'd been so sure that her brush with death would keep her safe and in her room—at least for tonight. He should have known better. As he saw her climb into her SUV, he reached for his coat. She had no business going out there alone—especially after what had happened to her tonight.

But at the same time, he wasn't at all surprised. She was one determined woman and he admired the hell out of her for that. Not that he was about to let her go alone.

As Hitch started to pull away, someone pounded on her window, startling her for a moment—until she saw Ford's handsome face. "Couldn't sleep again?" she asked.

"Felt like going for a ride. Looks like you had the same idea."

She studied him for a moment before she smiled. "All right. Get in."

He grinned as she unlocked the door and he climbed in.

"How are you feeling?" he asked.

"Fine."

"I thought you might have decided, after what happened to you, to stay in tonight," Ford said.

She glanced over at him as she pulled out and headed down the street toward the highway that would take them north. "No, you didn't or you wouldn't be here."

"Maybe I'd hoped you'd had enough for one day."

Hitch kept her attention on the road as they fell into a companionable silence until she turned off into the Collinwood Ranch. On the side of the mountain in the pines where they'd sat before, she cut the lights, pulled to the edge so there were no trees blocking their view and cut the engine.

"He wouldn't be fool enough to come back out here tonight," Ford said.

She chuckled. "Wanna bet?"

"I have a new twenty that says if he's the lover, he'll stay away."

Even in the dim starlight coming through the SUV's windows, she could see his smile. She liked that smile. "My twenty says the lover will visit tonight."

"Guess we'll see." He reached into his jacket pocket for his binoculars.

They sat quietly for a while. The pines stood in dark

shadow next to the vehicle while the landscape beyond the mountaintop was cast in a silver glow from the magnitude of the stars out here so far from town. She heard an owl hoot from a nearby tree, and somewhere farther off a hawk answered.

She turned the key to let down her side window, needing the cool summer night's air. Earlier at the hotel, she'd been so close to asking Ford into her hotel room. If she had, they wouldn't be here now. They'd be wrapped up in each other's arms. The thought sent a ball of heat straight to her center. And she knew the real reason she hadn't invited him into her room earlier.

Most men she could take or leave. Ford wasn't like that. She told herself she wasn't ready for the kind of commitment even one night with him might take. She had to keep her mind on this case, but it was hard to do that with Ford just inches away and this spark between them like a live wire.

"DOES IT WORRY you that just a few days ago I was ready to drive over a cliff?" Ford said inside the dark SUV. He thought that would give any woman pause, even one like Hitch. He had to know because he didn't want any secrets between them if they were going to become lovers. And he was pretty sure that they were.

"No, because you wouldn't have done it," she whispered, not looking at him.

He chuckled. "How can you be so sure?" he asked, turning toward her, studying the outline of her face in the darkness.

She turned to meet his gaze. "Because you didn't want to go over that cliff."

"I wish I believed that."

"Doesn't matter now anyway," Hitch said. "You're not in that state of mind anymore. You're not that man."

He smiled at her. "You know that how?"

She held his gaze. "I see it in your eyes. I also felt it in your kisses." She turned back to her surveillance. "You want to live."

Ford realized that she was right. He tried not to stare at her, even though he loved looking at her face, staring into her eyes. She had mesmerized him in a way that he thought could never happen to him again.

The pain of what he'd been through was still there and always would be. But Hitch had made him realize that he could go on. He might even be able to find happiness in this world he'd only seen as too broken to repair.

He cleared his throat, changing the subject. "Other than you losing twenty dollars, what if he doesn't show tonight?"

"I haven't lost yet. He can't stay away from her and they both know that a phone call will show up on their bills."

"You think it will go to trial?"

Hitch continued to study the ranch house for a long moment before she lowered her binoculars and answered. "If she suspects that could happen, she'll run before she's locked up."

The answer surprised him. "But the bond she put up—"

"I suspect she already planned to lose that and the ranch. It isn't the only money she has—you can bet on that. If she was smart, and she is, she would have planned this for some time and taken into account all possible outcomes. This wasn't an impulsive act. Who knows how long she's been hiding money for the day when she might need it? She could have been planning this for years. She thought of *almost* everything. What worries me now is what she plans to do with her accomplice."

Ford shot her a look. "You think she'll kill him."

"She doesn't have much choice. He keeps going off script. She can't trust him. He's too much of a liability. She's already killed her husband. What's one or two more murders," Hitch said as the garage door at the ranch house suddenly rolled up and Rachel's SUV rolled out.

"One or two more?" Ford said.

Hitch met his gaze. "If she thought you might change your story about what you heard on the phone call, well, you'd be in the same boat. That's why the sooner you go back to Big Sky, the better off you'll be."

She started the patrol SUV's motor and took off down the mountain without headlights to follow Rachel—wherever she was headed at this time of the night.

"And you owe me twenty dollars," Hitch said as she raced after the disappearing taillights in the distance.

Chapter Twenty

Hitch had expected Rachel to turn toward town as soon as she drove off the dirt ranch road. To her surprise, the SUV turned right at the highway and headed in the direction of Harlowton.

"Where is she going?" Ford said, sounding as surprised as Hitch was.

"Wherever it is, she's going there in a hurry." By the time Hitch reached the end of the ranch road and turned onto the highway headed north, she could barely see Rachel's taillights in the distance. "I think she's trying to lose us."

Turning on her headlights and tromping on the gas, she raced after her. While it had been Rachel's SUV that had come out of the garage, Hitch hadn't been able to see the driver. What if it wasn't Rachel behind the wheel?

Clouds had moved in, cloaking the night. Ahead, she could make out the dim taillights. Rachel, or whoever, was driving fast as if she knew she was being followed. Hitch didn't want to lose her, but she also didn't want to come running up on her in the growing fog and careen into the back of her vehicle either. As the terrain became more hilly, she only got glimpses of the blurry red taillights ahead of her through the fog.

Hitch was going eighty-five when she came up a hill and saw brake lights off to the side of the road. She recognized the SUV. The driver had pulled off onto a wide spot.

As Hitch sped past, she glanced at the driver of the SUV. Rachel was behind the wheel. She caught a glimpse of the woman's face and the smug smile plastered on it. As Hitch kept going, she watched in her rearview mirror as Rachel turned back toward the ranch.

Over the next hill, Hitch hit her brakes and did a highway patrol turn in the empty road before heading back to Big Timber. Ahead, she could see that Rachel was no longer speeding. Hitch followed her until she turned into her own ranch road.

"Was that what I think it was?" Ford said.

"She tricked me. Got me to follow her while whoever was visiting her got away," Hitch said. She had to hand it to the woman. Rachel had been one step ahead of her from the beginning. The subterfuge only made Hitch more convinced that the woman was guilty of cold-blooded murder.

Hitch just had to prove it, and that was the problem.

It was late by the time they reached the hotel.

"I don't know about you, but I could use a drink," Ford said and glanced at his phone. "Bar closes in less than an hour."

She smiled. "I thought you didn't drink."

"Only on special occasions."

"And you think this is one of them?" she asked with a chuckle.

"It just might be." His look said he wasn't ready to go to his hotel room alone. She knew the feeling. Maybe tonight they needed each other. She realized with a start that she more than needed him. She wanted him, which was entirely different. This kind of want made her ache inside.

The bar was empty except for a few regulars watching TV at the other end of the room. She ordered herself a screwdriver. Ford raised a brow and laughed and said he'd take the same. Taking a sip of her drink, she slid off the stool, went to the jukebox and punched in a few of her favorite songs.

The bartender saw her and turned down the volume on the TV as she took her stool again and the first song came on.

"Seriously, why are you involved in such a dangerous job?"

"Someone has to do it. I would think you'd know better than anyone why I do this."

"That was war. This is…"

"Its own kind of war," she said and ran a finger down the sweating fog on her glass. "I'm sorry I suspected you."

"Thanks, since I take that to mean you no longer do," he said.

"Do you still love her?" She hadn't meant to ask the question, but once it was out of her mouth, she was anxious to hear his answer. She hated that she was hanging on his answer, knowing he would be truthful with her.

He took a sip of his drink and chuckled to himself. "No. I've realized that I've never been in love with Rachel. Not the real kind. I was in love with the idea of her." He met her gaze. "But I'm not even in love with that anymore."

"Good," she said as a new song began on the juke-box.

Ford stepped off his stool. "Dance with me." He reached for her hand. His large one was warm and dry. A strong hand. It wrapped around hers as he gently led her out onto the small dance floor. A strong man, she thought as he took her in his arms.

They began to move to the slow country song. She breathed in the distinct male scent of him and was tired enough that she was almost tempted to rest her head on his shoulder.

She drew back a little to look into his face. "I'm serious about you leaving town."

He grinned. "Otherwise you won't be able to resist me?"

"Something like that. Ford, I'm serious. It's too dangerous. She saw us together tonight." She leaned back a little to meet his gaze. "Promise me that you'll leave in the morning."

"If that's what you want." He pulled her closer. This time she didn't resist. She rested her head on his shoulder, relishing being wrapped in his protective strength. What was it about this man that brought out such powerful feelings in her? It had happened so quickly that it had caught her off guard.

The song ended. When she raised her head from his shoulder, she met his gaze. Heat speed-raced through her veins, reminding her how long it had been since she'd even dated.

"Ford?"

"I know," he said. "Maybe when this case is over, if you—"

"I thought I'd find you here," said a deep male voice behind them.

Hitch turned to see the sheriff, thumbs hooked in the pockets of his jeans, his chest puffed out. "That lab of yours is trying to find you."

Chapter Twenty-One

When Hitch pulled out her phone, she saw that she had several messages from the DCI lab—and the governor. "I'm sorry. I have to go take care of this," she told Ford. Their gazes locked. "Thank you for the dance."

"We'll have to do it again sometime," he said with a slight bow of his head.

The look in his eye made her cheeks actually flush. "I hope so."

She rushed upstairs to the quiet of her room to listen to her messages. She desperately needed a break in this case and soon. She wanted this one over for more reasons than ever before.

After closing her door to the quiet of her room, she listened to the governor's first message. Bart Collinwood had been kicking up a lot of dust and so had Lloyd Townsend. If Hitch didn't find something solid on the case soon…

She listened to the DCI investigator's message and held her breath. Maybe this was the break she needed. "I have news, just not the news I think you were hoping to hear. We found no blood or tissue evidence on the ring to suggest it had been used in a violent attack. Nothing on the ring matched Rachel Collinwood's DNA either."

Hitch let out the breath she'd been holding and told herself it had been a long shot. Still, when she'd seen the Townsends' rings, she'd thought she'd found a clue. Those grooves were so deep in that design that something would have been found. And Rachel and Paul had been lovers. She'd thought she'd found the key to breaking this case wide open.

"As for the design and the bruise left on Rachel Collinwood's face, we ran both the ring and photo through a variety of tests. Our conclusion? It doesn't match. There are parts of it that are close... Sorry. We have a unit coming out your way tomorrow. I'll have them return the ring to you."

Hitch tossed her phone on the bedside table. She couldn't help but feel even more deflated. She'd been so sure that she'd found the accomplice. The ring that had made the bruise wasn't Paul Townsend's ring— nor was it the husband's. All Hitch had to do was find the ring that matched that bruise. Talk about looking for a needle in a haystack.

Another dead end. All her instincts told her that her suspicions weren't wrong. But unless she found evidence... Worse, when she thought about it, Paul Townsend was too young and too undisciplined to be the accomplice. Wasn't that why a year ago Rachel had cut him loose? Rachel had realized that she couldn't count on him. So who had she turned to?

As she got ready for bed, her thoughts kept straying to Ford. She'd met few men who could occupy her thoughts as much. She thought about what he'd confessed to her about the day he'd gotten the call from Rachel. It hadn't been easy for him to admit. She could tell that he was embarrassed by even the foiled attempt to end his life. She couldn't imagine how low he'd been at that moment to even consider it. Ford Cardwell wasn't the impulsive type. If suicide had been his intention, then Rachel really could have saved his life.

If so, then Hitch now believed in fate.

She realized that she had no solid proof that Rachel had planned the killing of her husband. That was what frustrated her the most. She had the lack of finger-prints on the glass and pottery. She had the lack of the husband's voice on the call to Ford. She had the bruise. She had the cartridge casing by the kitchen door. She had the lack of bruises and abrasions on the husband's hands. But even with all of that, it still might not be enough to hold up in court.

Had she lost her perspective? Had she wanted Rachel to be guilty? "What if your instincts are wrong?" she asked herself in the empty hotel room.

"I'm not wrong." Whatever Rachel had been hit with, it also hadn't been with her husband's ring. So whose had it been?

Whoever had hit her had forgotten to take off his ring. But Rachel would have realized it at some point and had him put Humphrey's ring on. Which meant Humphrey was already dead.

But without that ring… This was the part of a case that she hated the most. Being so close she could feel it, but not being able to find that one crucial piece of evidence that would complete her investigation. She'd been here before. Usually, it was something small that she'd overlooked. Or a mistake the criminal had made or was going to make.

She needed the accomplice—and that ring.

She climbed into bed, telling herself she'd never get to sleep, not with her roiling emotions—and her growing feelings for Ford Cardwell.

A few hours later, she was startled awake by the ringing of her phone. She picked up. "Good morning, Governor."

"Is it? What have we got on this investigation?"

"Nothing definite yet, but—"

"The sheriff seems to think that you're on some kind of crusade against this woman."

Hitch groaned inwardly. "I'm just trying to get at the truth like I always do."

"You have a great record at doing just that. But this case is…"

"Complicated."

"That's one way of putting it," the governor said. "I can't give you much more time on this. I have another case you're needed on. Not to mention the fact that you seem to have stirred up a hornet's nest."

"Give me forty-eight hours. If I don't have evidence by then, I'll leave it to the sheriff." Hitch knew what that would mean. Rachel Collinwood would get away with murder.

"Forty-eight hours."

The clock was ticking.

FORD WAS WAITING for Hitch when she came out of the hotel. He pulled her aside behind a pillar at the edge of the building. "You okay?" he asked, his hand still on her arm. She nodded, but he could tell something was wrong. "It wasn't the ring, was it," he said.

She groaned. "You know about the ring?" Shaking

her head, she said, "These small towns. No. It wasn't the ring I was looking for. I'd hoped it matched a bruise on Rachel's face." She described the bruise. "It didn't match close enough. So I'm back to square one, since I'm almost positive the bruise was made by a man's ring—just not her husband's."

Ford had heard about Paul Townsend being brought in. It had been his pickup that they'd seen leaving the Collinwood Ranch. But not his ring.

"I have an idea," he said, having given this some thought last night after they'd parted. He couldn't leave town. Not now. "Rachel trusts me. Put a wire on me and let me try to get the truth out of her."

Hitch was shaking her head before he could even finish speaking. "Not happening. I need to wind this investigation up in the next forty-eight hours, and quite frankly, you've become a distraction I can't afford."

"Is that what I am to you?" he said, grinning.

"I'm serious. Please go home so I know you're safe."

"I can't do that." He held her gaze. "I came here to save Rachel if I could. Instead, I find myself getting involved with you."

"I wouldn't say we're involved."

"Wouldn't you?" He cupped her cheek, drawing her face up to his own. "Tell me there is nothing between us and I'll walk away right now."

She parted her lips, but no words came out. He pulled her into his arms. He could feel her heart pounding in her pulse. "Last chance," he said.

Chapter Twenty-Two

Hitch had flat-out refused to even think about his plan. She was determined that he leave and go back to Big Sky. Did she really believe that Rachel would harm him? Kill him? Even if she'd murdered Humphrey, Ford didn't believe that she would kill him.

But he could also be wrong about that. Wrong about a lot of things when it came to Rachel. He knew it was risky. The thought made him laugh. It wasn't that long ago that he was racing toward a cliff with only one thought in mind—ending his life as he knew it.

Now, though, his life felt precious. He didn't want it to end. He wanted to live—even if Hitch Roberts wasn't part of it. Not that he was ready to give up on the two of them. She needed this investigation over and so did he. He could tell that she'd hit a wall in the investigation. If he could move it along, he would do whatever he had to.

As he drove out to Rachel's ranch, he told himself that maybe Rachel didn't trust him as much as she used to. But she didn't see him as a real threat. She saw him as naive and weak because of his feelings for her, which he'd more than demonstrated at her wedding. If anything, she found him dispensable, just as she had fifteen years ago. Now that he'd already given his state-ment to the sheriff, she wanted him gone.

But would she trust him enough to tell him the truth?

He had to pretend he was still blindly in love with her. That wouldn't be easy. Rachel had been his fan-tasy woman for years. Unfortunately, that woman had never existed, and it had taken her to show him that. Had Humphrey come to that same conclusion those last few seconds before she'd killed him?

Ford realized now that he'd used the fantasy of Ra-chel so other women never quite measured up and he didn't get hurt. As a boy, he'd seen the hell his father had gone through during the divorce. Ford's own mother had deserted them. No wonder he had commitment issues.

Until now. He'd never met anyone like Hitch before. She'd made him realize what he wanted in a woman— knocking Rachel off that pedestal he'd put her on.

As he pulled up in front of the ranch house, he knew this was going to have to be the acting job of his life. Rachel was smart. She was also leery of him after his last visit. If she spotted the lie… He pushed the thought away. He would just have to make sure she didn't.

As Rachel opened the door, he caught a whiff of fa-miliar perfume. Her hair was pulled up, a gold necklace twinkling at her slim throat. She was wearing a slinky jumpsuit in a turquoise blue that brought out the blue in her eyes and hugged her curves. The woman was drop-dead gorgeous and she knew it.

"Ford, I was glad when you called. Come in."

She let him into the living room. "I hate the way we left things the last time you were here." Soft music played in the background. The lights had been dimmed. "Have a seat. Let me get us something to drink."

Still standing, he watched her walk into the kitchen, taken aback by this warm reception. Earlier when he'd called, he'd said the same thing. He didn't like the way they'd left things. She'd sounded wary at best on the phone but had said of course she wanted to see him before he left.

Now he felt a sliver of concern work its way under his skin. This could be a huge mistake. But he was already here, he told himself as he looked around. He spotted Rachel's phone on the table next to the couch. Hadn't the sheriff taken her phone? This must be a new one. He realized that she must have been looking at it when he knocked and put it down and forgotten it.

Ford quickly picked it up. She hadn't signed off. He wasn't sure what he was even looking for. Certainly not a confession.

After glancing at her emails, he opened her photos. He went to the most recent ones. He was scanning through them when one caught his eye. All the breath rushed from him. It was of Rachel. She was tied to an iron bed, wearing nothing but what appeared to be a fireman's jacket that barely covered her private parts. He zoomed in to make the logo larger. Sweet Grass County volunteer fireman's jacket.

Had Humphrey been a local volunteer fireman? Ford knew it would be easy enough to find out, but he doubted it. In the photo, Rachel was laughing and saying something to the person taking the shot. It was the gleam in her eyes that told him the photographer wasn't Humphrey. That and the fact that this photo had been taken on her new phone, so it had been shot recently.

He quickly switched to open Rachel's contact list, curious about whose number he'd find, when she called from the kitchen.

"I hope you still like dark beer."

"You know me," he called back and quickly looked around for a place to put the phone. He stuffed it between two of the large, heavy fashion magazines on the coffee table as he heard her coming back and sat down next to it.

"I was so glad I had a beer for you," Rachel said, returning to the living room with a bottle of dark beer and a frosted glass, which she put down on the table at the far end of the couch next to him. She sat down at the opposite end of the couch, picked up her glass of red wine and turned toward him. Her smile looked glued on and slightly crooked. He figured it wasn't her first glass of wine tonight.

"I'm so sorry we had to reconnect after all these years in such a tragic way," she said. "It appears that all of Humphrey's and my dirty secrets are now local gossip. I'm so embarrassed."

"You shouldn't be embarrassed," he said. "I'm sure you never expected to find yourself in such a situation."

"Exactly," she agreed. "People like Humphrey and I… Well, I never expected something like this to happen. Not to us. I know you were shocked," she said, leaning toward him a little.

He got another wave of her perfume. It made him nauseous. He reached for his beer and poured some into the glass. The cold made him shiver a little. "I *was* shocked," he admitted. "I had no idea."

"No one did. Shyla said I should have told someone. Called the police on him. Done something more before things got totally out of hand." She shook her head and took a sip of her wine. Cupping the glass in her hands, she looked at him. "I was so ashamed. I didn't want anyone to know. I especially didn't want you to find out. What you must think of me."

"You can't believe that I would think less of you because of this."

Tears welled in all that blue. She licked her lips and gave him a sad smile. "You were Humphrey's best friend, but I always felt you and I... I don't know. That we had a special connection."

There would have been a time when those words would have warmed him to his toes. Instead, he found himself comparing this visit to the last one, when she'd been trying to get rid of him. Apparently, she wasn't hiding her boyfriend in the back bedroom this time.

"Ford, there's something I have to ask you." She put down her wineglass and turned all of her attention on him. "There's a rumor going around. I'm sure it's not true. Some people saw you dancing with that woman, the medical examiner, and the other night I went for a drive and..." Her gaze locked with his. "I thought I saw you in her patrol car."

"It's true," he said and picked up his beer as he broke eye contact with her. This part had to be the most convincing, so he took his time. "That's another reason I wanted to see you before I left." He took a drink and set down his glass to turn to her. "Rachel, I don't know how to tell you this." He could see that she was nervous and trying very hard not to show it. "Hitch, well... I suspect you already know that she doesn't believe your story."

"It wasn't a story," Rachel said automatically and

looked as if this wasn't news. She seemed to remember something. He saw her look around and frown. She was looking for her phone. He saw her glance toward the kitchen.

"Hitch says she has solid proof," he said, drawing her attention again. "That's why I wanted to see you, because I want you to know. I would do anything for you. I don't think it's a secret how I've always felt about you." He looked down as if embarrassed by his confession. "I always thought you and I..." He heard her move before he felt her hand on his arm.

"Ford. I've been so stupid from the very beginning. You were one of the few people who knew about my background, how poor I was, how scared I was of not having anything to call my own. I can't tell you how many times I've wished it had been you instead of Humphrey."

He looked into her eyes. The woman was amazing. So beautiful with her lips trembling like that and her eyes shimmering in tears. He'd always been so taken with her, never looking too deeply below the surface. Otherwise, he might have realized what an astonishing liar she was, he thought as he pulled her into his arms.

HITCH CAUGHT HERSELF pacing the floor as she read over the list of phone numbers she'd received from DCI of Rachel's calls to and from her cell phone as well as Humphrey's in the days that led up to the shooting.

No surprise, there were mostly calls to Humphrey's number and vice versa. Also, a lot of calls to her friend Shyla, who Ford had told Hitch about. She couldn't concentrate after Ford's message saying he was going out to the ranch. He would try to get Rachel to con-

fess on his phone. Did he have any idea how dangerous that could be if he got caught? She'd called him the
moment she'd gotten the text, but his phone had gone
straight to voice mail.

She kept thinking of the danger he was putting himself in. She should have stopped him. Or at least tried
harder to talk him out of what he was doing.

Rationally, she knew she couldn't have done either.

But she also couldn't sit around waiting to hear
from him. After seeing all the calls to the same number, she'd realized that she should talk to Shyla Birch,
allegedly Rachel's best friend. Not that she expected
to get anything from the woman. But she had to do
something.

Birch, who'd married a local deputy in town, lived
in a small house just outside of Big Timber. As Hitch
crossed the Yellowstone River, she caught sight of the
house and a flock of geese etched against the evening
sky. She hadn't called to see if Shyla was home, deciding to take a chance. She had, however, called to see
if the woman's husband was working tonight. He was.
She doubted Shyla would be forthcoming if there was
a deputy in the room.

Parking, she got out and headed for the front door.
She could smell the river. The night air had a wonder-
ful summer-is-coming feel to it. In Montana, summer
usually arrived somewhere before the Fourth of July
and ended shortly thereafter.

The woman who opened the door wasn't what Hitch
had been expecting. She was wearing a too-large T-shirt
and shorts. Her red curly hair formed a halo around her
head, accentuating large brown eyes. Her feet were

bare and she was holding a bowl of what smelled like buttered popcorn.

"Shyla Birch? I'm state medical examiner Hitch—"

"I know who you are," the woman said, tucking the large bowl of popcorn against her hip.

"Ford suggested I talk to you."

Surprisingly, those words seemed to do the trick. Hitch saw the woman hesitate and then sigh before she said, "Come on in, then."

The house smelled of stale cigarettes and popcorn. Shyla motioned to a chair by the couch as she grabbed the remote and muted the television before curling back under the blanket lying on the couch, with the bowl of popcorn in her lap. "Ford tell you that I'm Rachel's friend?"

"He said you were her *best* friend." That seemed to please her, Hitch saw, as she took the chair. "That's why I wanted to speak with you."

"I wondered when you'd get around to me." She shoved a handful of popcorn into her mouth.

"You probably know, then, what I'm going to ask you," Hitch said.

"Did I know he was abusing her? Did I see bruises? Did she ever talk to me about it?"

"And?" She waited for the young woman to answer.

Shyla pulled a face and put down the bowl of popcorn on the couch next to her as she picked up her cigarettes from the end table next to her. Hitch watched her light one and take a long drag before tilting her head back to let out a stream of smoke.

"She didn't tell me, but I saw bruises once or twice. She always had a story for how she'd gotten them. Looking back, though, oftentimes Humphrey would be there when she told me, so she was clearly covering for him and he was letting her."

"So you weren't surprised when you heard what had happened."

"Actually…" Shyla stared down at her cigarette for a moment. "I was shocked. I thought they were happy—in their own way. Did Ford tell you that I met my husband through Rachel?"

"No, he didn't. How did that come about?" she asked, trying hard not to sound like a medical examiner on a case. She must have succeeded, because Shyla seemed to relax a little, loosening up.

"Rick had gone out to the ranch after Rachel had called about a possible break-in. She'd come home and the front door was standing open. Humphrey was in New York on business and she was scared out of her wits. She called me to come out while she was waiting locked in her car." Shyla chuckled. "And the rest is history, as they say. Although I never thought I'd fall for a lawman." She rolled her eyes. "No offense."

"None taken. So had the house been broken into?"

"That's what's so weird. The door must have not been locked properly and had simply blown open. Rick had been going off shift when he got the call, so he stayed around to keep us company. Rachel made us some drinks. Humphrey came home and it kind of turned into a party. By the end, I was in love."

"Sounds like it was meant to be."

Shyla nodded, finished her cigarette and stubbed it out. "I heard that you think Rachel planned the whole thing."

There was something in the way she said it that made Hitch wonder if she also had thought the same thing. "I suspect she might have." She waited for a few moments before she added, "What do you think?"

Reaching for the popcorn bowl, Shyla took her time picking out a few kernels before she finally answered—instead of instantly defending her best friend.

"Rach is amazing. She really is. Did you know that she came from nothing? I mean, we were poor. Well, maybe not *poor* poor, but my parents both worked. They paid for my college, though, not like Rachel, who was on loans and scholarships. I don't blame her for wanting more than she got out of life, you know?" Hitch nodded. "But…" She looked down at the piece of popcorn in her fingers and tossed it back into the bowl, wiping her hand on the hem of her T-shirt, her thoughts clearly elsewhere. "I never thought she really loved Humphrey. Oh, she wanted him, but if you've ever been in love…"

Hitch remembered being in Ford's arms. It was an unexplainable feeling, an amazing, scary-as-hell feeling.

"But that doesn't mean she planned the whole thing," Shyla said, looking uncomfortable.

"No, possibly not," Hitch agreed. "I suppose you know about the prenuptial agreement she signed?"

"That was Humphrey's father's doing. Bart never liked Rachel. He thought she was a gold digger."

"Still, the agreement aside, Rachel could have divorced her husband and walked away with a lot of money."

Shyla let out a bark of a laugh. "Not near enough for that woman's tastes." She seemed to bite her tongue. "I shouldn't have said that."

"It's okay. I've seen her closet." An uneasy silence

filled the room. "I have just one other question. I really appreciate your candor, and nothing you've said will go beyond this room. Is Rachel capable of putting together a plan to get rid of her husband and make it look like he was trying to kill her?"

Hitch knew she was putting the woman on the spot. Shyla's first instinct would be to protect her friend. And yet there was something refreshingly honest about the young woman.

"I'm not saying that's what happened," Shyla said carefully. "But Rachel... Well, she's always gone after what she wanted and not let anything stand in her way. She's definitely capable of doing anything she sets her mind to. She's got that kind of personality. But would she purposely kill her husband?" She gave a shake of her head. "Who does that?"

Someone cold-blooded enough that she wanted out but refused to give up the money, Hitch thought as she thanked Shyla and got to her feet. As she started toward the door, she heard a vehicle pull up. The front door flew open before she reached it and a handsome, broad-shouldered man in uniform came in and stopped dead at the sight of her.

"Rick, this is the medical examiner. She's looking into Rachel's case," Shyla said as she came off the couch. She sounded embarrassed and a little too anxious. "She was just leaving."

Rick Birch's brow furrowed. "Did you tell her that we're good friends with Rachel? With her husband, too, before all this?"

"Of course," his wife said quickly.

"Nice to meet you, Deputy Birch," Hitch said and started to step past him. He didn't move for a moment, blocking the doorway out. She continued toward him until he had to make a choice. He moved aside, but he didn't look happy about it.

On her way out the door, she heard him say, "What did you say to her?" before the door closed behind her.

Hitch walked to her car, thinking about everything she'd heard—and felt—from Rachel's best friend. Shyla had her doubts. Hitch wasn't the only one who suspected Rachel of far more than shooting her husband during a domestic dispute.

Climbing into her SUV, she started the engine and checked her phone, anxious to hear from Ford. She was getting even more worried after her talk with Shyla. She was about to pull out when her headlights glinted off something in the garage. She hit the brakes and stared at the small single-car garage attached to the Birch house. The garage door had a chunk missing where it appeared someone had driven into it. Through the opening, she saw what looked like the chrome of a cattle guard on the front of a pickup.

Putting the SUV into Park, she got out and walked to the garage door to look inside through the large hole. A pickup was parked inside. The large grille-guard bumper on the front was what had caught her eye. She stared at it, recognizing the design. It was exactly like the one that had nearly hit her the other night.

Chapter Twenty-Three

Rachel hugged him, pressing her breasts against him. He felt her hand move across his chest around to his side, down to his hip. He realized with a start that she had checked him for a wire. Then her hand slipped into his pocket of his jacket. It came back out with his phone.

She drew back, looked down at it in her hand and touched the screen. "Oh, I'm sorry. This is yours. I thought my phone must have slipped down between the couch cushions." She didn't hand the phone back as she moved to the middle of the couch and reached for her wineglass with her free hand. She took a sip before she set his phone down between them.

She looked around again. "I thought I left my phone in here."

"Your phone?" He pretended to look around for it, and as he sat up, he kicked the leg of the coffee table. "Oh, there it is." He'd sent one of her fashion magazines sliding to the edge of the table, exposing the phone he'd put there. "Is that it?"

She stared at the phone. He could see her trying to remember where she'd laid it down and if it could have gotten covered by a magazine.

He took advantage of her momentary confusion to continue what he was saying. "Hitch has discovered incriminating evidence against you. I tried to find out what it is, but she wouldn't tell me. I'm just afraid it's going to get you sent to prison for the rest of your life."

She picked up her phone, pocketing it before taking another sip of her wine. She grimaced as if it tasted bitter on her tongue and put down her glass. "Has she taken this evidence to the prosecutor?"

"I don't know. Rachel, you know how I feel about you. Is there anything I can do?"

"Having you here, it's meant so much to me. I'm surprised you've stayed this long." She studied him for a moment. "I need more wine," she said, getting to her feet. She picked up his empty beer bottle. "Can I get you another beer?"

"Sure," he said as she headed into the kitchen. He realized that from here he could see her in the mirrored cabinets across from the sink. He watched her lean against the granite counter as if she needed it for strength. With a shaking hand, she refilled her glass and got another beer for him out of the refrigerator.

It was what she did next that stopped his heart cold. She opened the beer, poured some into a new frosted glass from the refrigerator's freezer, and then she took a small vial from her pocket.

He watched in horror as she poured something into his beer, holding up the glass to the light to make sure it had dissolved. Calling from the kitchen, she said, "You know me so well. That's why I'm glad you're here. I can tell you the truth."

She smiled as she picked up his beer and her wine-glass. He watched her take a breath and then head into the living room.

IN THE LIVING ROOM, Ford quickly picked up his phone and hit Record. He put the phone back down where she'd left it and tried to still his breathing. His heart pounded so loudly, he feared she would be able to hear it. Of course Rachel was suspicious of his motives. But then again, he'd come running at the first sign that she was in trouble, reinforcing her belief that he adored her, that he'd always adored her, that he would always wish it had been him instead of Humphrey she'd fallen in love with. Did she think he was hoping for another chance with her, now that Humphrey was gone? Probably, knowing Rachel.

"Here," she said as she came back into the room and handed him the glass of beer.

He set the frosted glass with the doctored beer on the coffee table. Rachel quickly reached to put a coaster under it. "Thank you," he said but didn't touch the beer.

She returned to the kitchen to snag a full opened bottle of wine, then returned to her place at the end of the couch, facing him. "Humphrey loved a chilled glass for his beer, but I guess I don't need to tell you that. You probably remember."

He nodded. "I'm so sorry things turned out the way they did." She took a sip of her wine and didn't look at him. "I mean it, Rachel. If there is anything I can do… You know I'm here for you."

She looked up then, and their eyes locked for a few seconds before she said, "I wish there was, Ford. Having you here, it's meant so much to me. How will I ever be able to repay you?"

He thought about what he'd seen her put into his beer glass. Was it something that would kill him? Or just make him deathly ill? Gut-wrenching poison or truth serum? With Rachel, he had no idea.

One thing was clear. She hadn't bought his act.

"Remember the first time we met?" she was saying, a cheerfulness in her voice that didn't quite ring true. "I wish I could go back to that day. If you had left me alone, that squirrel would have eaten out of my hand."

He smiled in spite of himself. "Because you wouldn't have given up until it did. You were always like that. When you wanted something, you hung in until you got it."

"Like with Humphrey," she said, the cheerfulness gone. "You know he had second thoughts about marrying me, don't you? Of course you did. You were his best man, his best friend. He would have told you. He wouldn't have married me if it wasn't for the pregnancy. You probably thought that I got pregnant on purpose so he didn't get away. That's what his father thought. After we got married, when I lost the baby, Humphrey was devastated. He wanted that child so badly." She looked away as she took a sip of her wine. "I don't know why I'm bringing all of this back up. Bad memories."

"He loved you."

She met his gaze again. "Yes, he did. But he never forgave me." She let out a bitter laugh. "He would have left me, except that it would have proved his father right."

He frowned. "Forgave you for what?"

"I didn't lose the baby, because there never was one. His father hired a private investigator. I lied about the pregnancy. Humphrey didn't find out until we'd been married almost a year."

"What was the fight about the day he died?" Ford asked.

She looked away for a moment. "He found my birth control pills." She laughed. "Stupid me. I never kept them in my purse."

He stared at her in shock. "Why wouldn't you want his child? Wouldn't Bart have changed his mind about you if you'd given him a grandchild?"

"I wasn't anyone's broodmare," she snapped. "I wasn't ruining my figure, let alone having a child to take care of. That wasn't the life I wanted."

He didn't know what to say. His shock must have shown.

"Didn't I have the right? It's my body."

Ford couldn't help but wonder what his old friend would have done when he found out that his wife had been lying to him for years. "You could have adopted."

She let out a bitter bark of a laugh. "That's exactly what he said, telling me that we could adopt children no one else wanted because we had this amazing place to raise them." She looked horrified. "Children no one else wanted? Over my dead body."

Could her lies have led Humphrey to attack her? Maybe Rachel was telling the truth.

"Also, some money had gone missing from this foundation Humphrey had started. I was involved in it and he had the gall to ask me if I'd stolen it." She took another sip of her wine, anger pinching her classic features.

Ford let out the breath he'd been holding. Now he realized how little he'd known about their relationship or the lengths Rachel would go to get what she wanted. "Did he threaten divorce?"

Rachel laughed. "He said he needed time to think. That he still loved me. But that he couldn't look at me right then. He took off into town to see his girlfriend at the café. It doesn't matter if they were actually sleeping together," she snapped before Ford could correct her. "The girl was all doe-eyed around him. Just the kind of woman he'd thought he'd married."

"That sounds like Humphrey," Ford said. "The part about still loving you. He told me at the wedding that he suspected you were lying about the pregnancy and even why you wanted to marry him so badly, but he said he didn't care. He loved you."

Tears filled her eyes. "I never knew that." She looked away again and downed more of the wine. "I hate to imagine what you must think of me." Her gaze went to his beer glass sweating on the coaster on the coffee table. "You haven't touched your beer."

"Did you do it, Rachel? Did you stage the whole thing to get rid of him so you didn't lose the money?"

Her head jerked around so she was facing him again. Color rushed to her cheeks, anger glinting in her eyes. "That's what you think, isn't it? You and the medical examiner."

He couldn't deny it. "Is it true? It's just you and me here, Rachel. Tell me so I can help you."

She glared at him for a long moment before she put down her wineglass and rose to her feet. "I think you should leave."

He nodded. "Just one more question." He motioned

to the room, taking her in with it. "What did you hope to accomplish tonight with the dim lighting, the perfume, that silky outfit you're wearing and the chilled beer glass? Were you worried that you'd lost my undying admiration and love?"

She shook back a lock of her blond hair that had come loose and fallen around her face. Her blue eyes were hard as ice chips and just as cold. "You have always underestimated me, Ford. If I wanted to seduce you, we'd be in my king-size bed right now."

He smiled. "No, Rachel, this time, you overestimated yourself." He picked up his phone. Turning off the recording, he looked up at her. "I came out here hoping you would tell me the truth. After all, you pulled me into this." He glanced at his beer glass. "I can't even imagine what you put into my beer, but I know now that you used me—just like you did Humphrey until you got tired of him. Was he going to divorce you? Is that why you killed him?" Her answer was that icy glare. "I wasn't kidding about the medical examiner being on to you. You thought your old life was bad? Wait until you get to prison."

With that, he turned to walk out. The wineglass hit the wall next to him and shattered, red wine droplets splattering against the white wall like blood.

He turned to look back at her seething angry face. Was this the last thing Humphrey saw before she pulled the trigger?

HITCH WAS SO relieved when she opened her hotel room to find Ford standing there that she threw herself into his arms. He smiled as if touched by her concern and kissed her. They stayed like that for long minutes.

"She didn't buy it," he said as they moved deeper into her room. "But she did try to drug me."

"What?"

"I saw her put a powder substance in my second beer. But I did get something. She left her new phone in the room with me when she went into the kitchen. There was a recent photo taken of her tied to an iron bed. The only thing she was wearing was a Sweet Grass County Volunteer Fire Department jacket. It's her new phone, so the photographer wasn't Humphrey. She did it," he said quietly. "I know she did it. I saw it in her face." He sat down on the foot of her bed. "She killed him. She planned the whole thing right from the beginning fifteen years ago. I just don't know why she waited so long."

Hitch sat down next to him as he told her everything that had happened. Then he let her listen to the recording on his phone. When they'd finished, Hitch actually felt shocked. As long as she'd been in this business, she'd believed that she could no longer be shocked. "That woman is cold."

She got up and went over to the bed where the case notes were spread across the top. It took her only a moment to find what she was looking for. "The fingerprints found on the birth control pill package on the floor were Humphrey's."

He turned to her. "She admitted that's what they fought about. So maybe he didn't threaten her with divorce and she saw only one way to have it all. You have to stop her. No matter what it takes. She can't get away with this."

She smiled at him. "Don't worry. I'm working on it." She told him about her visit to Shyla Birch's house and meeting her unfriendly husband, the deputy, along with what she'd found in the garage.

Ford's eyes widened in alarm. "Are you telling me the pickup that almost killed you was driven by a deputy?"

"Or his wife. *Possibly.* The problem is the grille guard on the front of the pickup. When I got back, I found the manufacturer. The company sold nine in this area. *Nine.* But I can tell you one thing. Rick Birch and his wife are both with the Sweet Grass County Volunteer Fire Department. I saw one of their jackets hanging by the door as I left—not that it narrows it down. A lot of locals are also volunteer firemen. So tell me what you know about Shyla."

He raked a hand through his hair. "She was impulsive and a little wild, but I can't imagine her trying to run you down."

"I agree. Between the two? I would pick the husband."

Ford let out a curse. "You think he's Rachel's accomplice?"

"I think it's possible." She told him the story Shyla had related to her about how they'd met and fallen in love. "She credits Rachel for getting them together."

"You think Rachel knew him before then?"

Hitch shrugged. "I suspect he's protective of Rachel. He wasn't happy to see me with his wife. As I was leaving, I heard him demand to know what she said to me. He seems like the kind who went into law enforcement to bust heads. If he bought into Rachel's story about her husband, he might have seen helping her as a way to right a wrong. Or he could just be sleeping with her and agreed to do whatever she asked him to."

"He's *married* to Shyla."

Hitch rolled her eyes. "Right, Rachel's so-called best friend. You really think that would stop him?"

Ford shook his head. "How are you going to prove it one way or the other?"

"I wish I knew. The fact that he's a deputy makes it harder."

"But if you told the sheriff about the truck that tried to run you down…"

She saw realization sink in before he could finish. "Exactly. My word against his deputy. In the first place, I can't prove it was even him, let alone that he was trying to kill me. Nor did I get a license plate number. Just a metal guard like at least eight others like it around… So even if I could put his pickup on that street that night definitively, he could say that he never saw me. It is a very dark street."

"What are you going to do?" he asked, his voice softening as he looked at her.

She shook her head. "I'm just glad that you're all right."

"I'm sorry it didn't work. Rachel's too smart for me."

Hitch laughed. "She's not too smart for either of us and she's going to prove it. She has to be rattled right now. I would think she'll be contacting her accomplice."

"Another night on the mountain?"

"Not this time," Hitch said. "I have her phone tapped. We should be hearing something soon."

He tucked a lock of her hair behind her ear. "What should we do in the meantime?"

RACHEL HAD STORMED around her house after Ford left. Who did he think he was? That he'd come out to her house to try to get her to admit to something she hadn't done? What kind of friend was that?

She stopped to stare at the wall, still red from her wine, the broken glass twinkling on the carpet, and she felt all the anger rush from her. Stumbling back to the couch, she looked for her phone until she realized she'd put it in her pocket earlier. Frowning, she glanced at the coffee table. The magazines were no longer neatly displayed, but they had been before Ford arrived. So how could her phone have gotten under one of them?

It couldn't have.

She felt an icy chill run like spider legs down her spine and shuddered. He'd had her phone. She opened it. A photo came up of her on the bed and she dropped to the edge of the couch. With trembling fingers, she placed the call.

"Rachel, what's wrong?" Shyla said when she answered and heard her crying. "Do you want me to come out there?"

"No," Rachel said quickly. "It's… Ford was here earlier. He said some awful things to me."

"Like what? Rachel? Did I lose you? Are you still there?"

"It's my new cell phone. I don't know what's wrong with it. The battery keeps running down. I'm plugging it in. Just a minute."

"Rach," Shyla said when she came back on. "Rick is standing here. He wants to talk to you."

"Did I hear you're having trouble with your new cell phone?"

"I can't seem to keep it charged."

Rick let out a curse. "Rachel, they've got your phone tapped. The taps run down the batteries. Have you seen any apps that have suddenly appeared that aren't yours?"

She gritted her teeth and tried not to snarl. "I've had a little too much on my mind to be checking my *apps*."

"What about any weird text messages?"

Rachel opened her mouth to snap at him but closed it. "I got something about winning a prize that I had to redeem."

He swore. "Is your phone warmer than your old one? They often overheat if someone is using GPS to track your phone." She said it was. "Which means they're not just tapping into your calls—they're tracking you."

Rachel felt her skin grow clammy and cold. "What can I do?"

"Get rid of any apps you don't recognize, then update your phone and don't use it."

"And how am I supposed to hear from you?" she cried.

"I'll get you a burner. I'll have Shyla bring it out. But you have to quit running scared and acting like you're guilty. Remember, you're the victim here. Humphrey would have killed you."

She nodded as she looked at the wine staining her wall. "Rick, I'm scared."

"Don't be. You did what you had to do. They're just trying to rattle you. Shyla wants to talk to you."

"Are you sure you don't want me to come out there?" her friend asked.

"No," Rachel said, looking at her phone where she'd plugged it in. "I'm fine. I'm going straight to bed. I think I just need a good night's sleep." She disconnected, and picking up Ford's beer where he'd left it, she walked into the kitchen and poured it down the drain.

For a moment, she stood at the sink staring out into the darkness before she walked down to her bedroom and began to pull out her luggage.

Chapter Twenty-Four

"So you're really going," Hitch said the next morning when she woke up next to Ford. She'd been encouraging him to go for days. She'd seen the change in him, though, last night. He was finally free of Rachel Westlake Collinwood. She wished she was.

Last night after their lovemaking, Ford opened up to her. They'd shared stories, confided hopes and dreams and fears. Then they'd made love again and held each other like two lost souls caught in a storm.

"I need to go back and figure out what I'm going to do for a living," he said. "But I'm only a phone call away." He smiled at her and she felt the heat of it race through her veins. Last night had been amazing. Ford was a tender, thoughtful lover who took it slow—the first time. She smiled to herself, remembering the passion of the second time. Her cheeks heated at the memory.

"I'll miss you," she said, snuggling against him.

"No, you won't. You'll be too busy getting to the truth."

"I wish, but the forty-eight hours the governor gave me is almost up. On top of that, the sheriff told the governor about us. Not that I care," she was quick to add. "It just…"

"Complicates things. Another reason I need to leave."

Unfortunately, she had to agree, especially after what Ford had told her about Rachel trying to drug him. "This investigation has to break soon."

He laughed. "You'd know better than me, but I sure hope so."

"I have just a little more time before I have to put this one behind me. But just the thought of turning it over to the sheriff… As if he's going to continue gathering evidence between now and the trial. If there even is a trial." She shook her head. "So basically, nothing will be done, and Rachel will either get off entirely or receive a light sentence. There's nothing I can do about it."

Ford pulled her closer. "You still have a little time."

She chuckled. "At this point, I could have a month and I'm not sure I'd know exactly what happened on that ranch that day. And the worst part is that if I'm right that is exactly what Rachel is counting on."

He kissed her passionately before he let her go. "I'll call when I get back to Big Sky. Once you wrap it up—"

"The governor said there's another case waiting for me. But don't worry. I'll find a way to see you." Because she couldn't bear the thought of being away from him very long.

He pulled her closer. "I can't wait for you to meet my family."

She felt at a loss for words, wanting to tell him how she felt, but knowing that the timing was wrong. "We'll talk soon."

FORD KNEW IT was time to go home. He could tell during his father's last call that he was getting worried. It was Rachel. Jackson worried that he was too involved in this case—if not involved with Rachel herself.

Mostly, Ford knew he had to let Hitch do what she did so well and quit distracting her. She couldn't do her job if she was worried about him. He'd played amateur detective, and if he hadn't seen whatever Rachel had put in his beer, he would be buried now in the garden on the ranch.

He was on the edge of Big Timber leaving town when his cell phone rang. He saw it was Rachel calling and almost didn't take it. "Rachel?" For a moment, he didn't hear anything but crying. Then he heard the words that had him hitting his brakes and pulling to the side of the road.

"You're right about me. I don't deserve to live," Rachel said, her words slurred as if she were drunk. Drunk? Or drugged?

"What's going on?" he asked, his pulse jumping at her words.

"I can't do this anymore," she said. "I should have told you everything last night. I should have… I can't live with myself…" She began to sob again.

"Have you taken something, Rachel?" He heard her drop the phone, the rest of her words inaudible.

Swearing, he quickly turned around and headed toward the ranch. He debated calling 911 for an ambulance, but he was already on his way and would be there in a matter of minutes at this speed. Maybe she was just drunk. But if she'd taken something… He thought of that time in college when she and Humphrey had a fight and she'd taken a bottle of pills. Ford and

Humphrey had walked her for hours until she came
out of it.

He was just north of town near the creek when he
caught lights in his rearview mirror. A highway patrol cruiser came racing up behind him, siren blaring,
lights flashing. Ford swore but pulled over, planning
to tell the officer why he'd been speeding and ask for
his help. Rachel would hate that he brought the cops
into it, but he had no choice now. He reminded himself that this was the woman who'd planned to drug
him just last night. Still, he didn't want her overdose
death on his conscience. Nor did he want Hitch's case
to end like this.

When he started to pull over, the cruiser drew up
beside him. The officer behind the wheel motioned
for him to pull off the road onto a side road. He did as
ordered, anxious to talk to the cop. He could feel the
clock ticking and thought about calling 911 but knew
it would take too much explanation. Pulling out his
phone, he quickly called Hitch, but before he could
speak, the officer tapped on his window.

Ford whirred down his window. "Officer, I know I
was speeding," he said to the sandy-haired young cop.
He saw that he was a deputy sheriff—not highway patrol as he'd first thought. "I just got a call—"

"Please get out of your vehicle."

"What? No, you don't understand." His pulse jumped.
Something was wrong. His gaze went to the man's hands
resting on the edge of the open window. A large ring on
the officer's right hand caught his eye. Something about
the design… He heard Hitch's voice far away and realized that she was still on the phone. "Officer, Rachel

Collinwood called. I was on my way there before you pulled me over here by the creek—"

"I said get out of your vehicle now!"

"Okay, but this is highly unusual. Kind of like your ring…" He spotted the man's name on his shirt. "Officer Birch." His heart was now a hammer in his chest. Shyla's husband. The ring. The grille guard on the pickup that tried to run Hitch down. "I feel as if I've seen that ring before," he said, praying that Hitch was still on the line, that she was hearing this.

Movement in his side mirror. "Rachel? No wonder you weren't worried about her. She just climbed out of your patrol car."

"What the hell?" Birch said and spotted the phone lying on the seat next to Ford. The cop leaned in, snatched the keys from the ignition and, shoving Ford back, scooped up the phone. He swore and quickly ended the call, but hopefully Hitch had heard it all.

HITCH HAD BEEN going through the evidence on the Collinwood case when she'd gotten Ford's call. "Hello? Hello?" She could hear Ford talking and realized he wasn't talking to her but to someone else. As his words registered and the call ended, she threw down the photos she'd been studying, grabbed her gun and her purse, and raced out to her patrol SUV, her heart in her throat.

Her mind whirred as she played what she'd heard over and over again. He'd been headed for Big Sky. But Rachel had called. Whatever she'd said had him headed for her ranch, where he was pulled over by Officer Rick Birch. Why had Birch pulled him over by the creek? And why was the deputy demanding Ford get out of the car? As Ford said, very unusual. And the ring…

She felt her pulse thundering through her veins. If she was right, Ford was in serious trouble. He'd passed as much of a message as he'd been able to before the call had been disconnected.

With her siren blaring and lights flashing, she sped out of town, across the bridge over the Yellowstone River, headed north. She had a pretty good idea of where Ford had been pulled over. He'd said by the creek. It was the turnoff to the Crazy Mountains. She zipped past several cars that had pulled over at the sound of her siren. She took a few curves and hit the brakes as she saw the turnoff ahead.

But she couldn't see if Ford's pickup and the deputy's cruiser were still parked down by the creek yet. It had taken her only minutes to get here, but what if she was too late?

"LET ME HANDLE THIS," Rachel said as she walked up to the driver's-side window and pushed the deputy aside.

"I see that you're feeling better," Ford said, wondering what these two thought they were going to do as he opened his glove box to take out his gun. With a sinking feeling, he saw that it was gone.

As he turned to look at her, Ford foolishly still believed that they weren't going to kill him. He heard the deputy come around to the passenger side of the pickup and open the door. They wouldn't kill him—not right here beside the main highway north. He turned back to Rachel, since she was clearly in charge, saw the expression on her face and knew that he was a dead man.

He had only a second to react. Way too little time to see the syringe in her hand before she stabbed the needle into the back of his shoulder. He tried to grab for it, but the deputy was on him, restraining him until she pulled the needle from Ford's flesh. By then, it was too late. He already felt the drug rushing through him.

"What the hell, Rachel?" he managed to say.

"Drag him over to the passenger side," Rachel said, reaching in to unsnap his seat belt. The deputy grabbed him. Ford tried to fight him off, but he could feel his muscles already going slack. "Now give me the keys and wait for me in your car for a moment."

Birch looked as if he didn't like taking orders from a woman, but with a grunt, he snapped Ford's seat belt in place, climbed out, slammed the passenger-side door and returned to his patrol car, parked behind Ford's pickup.

"Rachel?" He felt dizzy, his vision beginning to blur. Whatever she'd injected him with, it was fast acting. His fingers felt like they were no longer his own as he tried unsuccessfully to unhook his seat belt. He heard Rachel lock his door with the child safety lock system.

"Sit tight for a moment," she said and closed the driver's-side door. He could see her walking back to the cruiser in his side mirror.

Ford knew he had to do something, but with his coordination getting worse as the drug took hold, he realized even if he could get out of the pickup, he probably couldn't stand, let alone run.

At the sound of a gunshot, he flinched.

The driver's-side door of his pickup opened a moment later and Rachel climbed in.

"What did you do?" he asked, his words slurred. He tried to get his arms to move, thinking he would go for her throat, but both arms hung useless at his sides.

"*I* didn't do anything," she said as she wiped the

pistol in her hand clean with a handkerchief. He recognized it as his own gun. "*You* did." Then, taking his right hand, she pressed his palm, then trigger finger into the cold steel. Using the handkerchief, she tossed his gun behind the pickup seat.

When had she gotten it out of his glove box? Or had it been Birch who'd taken it on one of the occasions Ford had stopped by the ranch to see Rachel? Had she been planning this the whole time?

She started the pickup and headed down the dirt road toward the Crazy Mountains. He didn't bother to try to ask what she planned to do with him. His tongue felt too large and useless in his dry mouth to waste speech on a question when he already knew the answer. She planned to kill him—just as she had her accomplice.

HITCH RACED UP to the turnoff. It wasn't until she dropped off the highway into the creek bottom that she could see the sheriff's deputy's patrol cruiser still parked there. But there was no sign of Ford's pickup. She could, however, see that Deputy Birch was sitting behind the wheel.

She quickly pulled up behind the cruiser and, gun drawn, stepped out to cautiously approach. The deputy was wearing his Western hat. He appeared to be looking down at something in his lap. He didn't move as she inched along the driver's side of his vehicle.

As she drew nearer, she could see that his window was down. The summer breeze coming up off the creek was warm. It made a slight whistling sound through the patrol cruiser's antenna. Hitch came alongside, the weapon pointed at the man's head, and grabbed the door handle and pulled. It took her a moment before she realized that she wouldn't be needing her gun. Officer Rick Birch had already been shot in the side of the head.

Slamming the door, she looked up the road and spotted dust boiling up some distance away between her and the Crazies. She glanced around to see if there were fresh tracks where someone had turned around. There weren't.

Her nerves were taut as she rushed back to her rig, jumped in and took off. As she did, she called DCI and gave them the information as to where they would find sheriff's deputy Rick Birch. Disconnecting, she drove, following the dust trail, praying she was right about the vehicle kicking up the dust being Ford's pickup. If she was, then Rachel was with him. Which meant that if Ford was still alive, it wouldn't be for long.

Chapter Twenty-Five

"You wanted so badly to hear the truth?" She glanced at him before going back to her driving.

Ford saw the gleam in her blue eyes. She wanted to tell him. She wanted someone to know how clever she was.

Rachel suddenly hit the brakes so hard that even with his seat belt on, he flew forward. She caught him before his head hit the dash. "You're not wearing a wire, are you? Surely there wasn't time after my call." She tore open his shirt, checked under the waist of his jeans and then behind him before she sighed. "Of course you're not. And I have your phone. Even if I didn't, you wouldn't be able to record me." She laughed as she got the truck going again.

"You want my confession? You got it. I killed him. I set the whole thing up. It wasn't that hard," she said, warming to her story as she drove through the foothills toward the mountains. "I planned it for months, stashing away any money I could get my hands on. When he found the birth control pills... Well, I hadn't planned on that. He was so furious. I realized he really might divorce me. I followed him into town. I knew he'd go to that girl. I wanted to have the argument at her house.

I wanted people to see it. Then I drove home. I'd already torn up the kitchen, breaking everything by the time he came home from town."

He thought about how Humphrey's fingerprints hadn't been found on any of the broken dishes on the floor—a red flag that Hitch had picked up on right away. If he had torn up the kitchen, his prints would have been on at least some of the shards. He wanted to tell her that it had been one of several mistakes she'd made, including killing Birch—and now him, but he could no longer speak. All he could do was listen and pray that Hitch had gotten the messages he'd tried to pass.

"You should have seen Humphrey's face when he walked into the kitchen and saw the mess. He actually looked at me as if I'd lost my mind. He really thought it was about that waitress at the café in town." She laughed. "He was going to help me clean up the mess. But before he could pick up anything, I jabbed him with the syringe—just like I did you." She chuckled. "It's fast acting, as you know, but he still managed to take a couple of steps toward me, so I pulled the gun. He looked dumbfounded for a moment, then demanded I hand the gun over." Her smile sent ice down his spine. It was worse than her laugh. "Oh, I gave it to him, all right."

"So you shot him before you pretended to be beaten by him." His words came out so slurred, he couldn't imagine how she had made sense of them.

"Pretended to be beaten?" she demanded. "Are you serious? You saw how badly I was injured." She sounded as if for a moment she believed her own lies.

"Rick got a little carried away. I told him to make it look real. He certainly did that."

But he'd forgotten to take off his ring. Rachel must have noticed at some point. That would have been when they took off Humphrey's ring and the deputy used it to hit her. He'd seen the deputy's ring only minutes ago and recognized it from the bruise photo Hitch had shown him this morning, asking if he'd seen a ring that could have made that mark.

"That was the tricky part," Rachel was saying. "I needed someone I could trust. Rick was more than up for the job. But the fool actually thought that we would be together once I was exonerated."

Ford thought of Paul Townsend. How many other men had Rachel "interviewed" for the job before she got the deputy to help her?

She gave a slight shrug as if Birch had been dispensable, just like Humphrey. He felt his anger, once molten with rage, stir in him, cold as this woman. He knew he could kill. He had in the war. He wished he could get his hands around Rachel's neck right now. She hadn't given a thought to her best friend, Shyla.

"You probably are wondering where you came in," Rachel said to him as the foothills were behind them and he was looking out at the mountain road ahead.

HITCH SAW THE vehicle still a long way ahead of her slow and turn. She felt relief wash over her. It was Ford's pickup—just as she'd thought. Her instincts had been right. She called for backup, explaining that Deputy Birch had been shot and killed and that Rachel Collinwood appeared to have taken Ford Cardwell captive. They were now headed into the Crazy Mountains. She gave the dispatcher the name of the road they were on and disconnected as Ford's pickup disappeared into the pines as it headed up the mountainside.

She told herself that Ford was still alive. She had to believe that. Rachel hadn't killed him and wasn't only driving up into the mountains to dump the body. If she'd done that, she would have needed the deputy's help. So what was her plan?

The deeper they got in the mountains, the more worried she became. She felt helpless because no matter what she did, it might only put Ford in more danger. Rachel had already killed twice. There was nothing keeping her from killing again.

All she could assume was that Rachel planned to end it and take Ford with her. The woman couldn't possibly think that she could still get away with what she'd done, could she? Probably, Hitch realized, remembering Rachel's arrogance.

As she closed the distance between her rig and the pickup, Hitch worried that Rachel would spot her. The mountain road, bordered on each side by pines, climbed in a series of switchbacks up the steep peak.

Hitch had lost sight of the pickup as she drove up the road in the shadow of the mountain. Her heart was thundering in her chest. She could feel the clock ticking. If Ford was still alive… She sped up, realizing she couldn't be that far from the top.

RACHEL'S VOICE BECAME an annoying drone in his ears as he listened to how cleverly she'd planned to kill her husband. "So Humphrey's lying on the floor dead. Rick has finished beating me when I call you, Ford. I scream and cry and finally grab the gun and fire a shot out the open kitchen door and disconnect, tossing it into Humphrey's blood and my own on the floor. I wait until Rick is gone before I call 911."

She didn't know about the cartridge casing Hitch had found just outside the kitchen door that had fallen through the deck slats. He made a disgusted, pained sound, thinking of his once best friend and this woman who'd come between them. She'd killed Humphrey, her deputy lover, and now she was about to kill him—unless somehow she was stopped.

He tried to ask if it was worth it, but nonsense came out of his mouth. She didn't seem to be listening anyway. What galled him was that she really thought she was going to get away with all of it—and she just might.

Unless Hitch had gotten the message he'd tried to pass to her. Hopefully she'd heard enough of the phone conversation to figure it out. If anyone could, it would be her, he thought, his heart aching. He'd found her and now would lose her. But he knew that Hitch wouldn't rest until she took Rachel down for all of it.

Rachel would never see the outside again. She'd told him that she'd worried about her next meal as a child. She wouldn't have to worry about it in prison. Nor about what to wear. And she deserved everything she would get and more.

"You probably want to know if I took the foundation money," she said as she drove up the mountain road. "I had no choice. Humphrey had cut off most of my credit cards and threatened to put me on a budget. I'm sure it was his father's idea. I had already lived hand to mouth. I wasn't going to do that again." She looked at him. "I suppose you'd say I could have gotten a job."

She scoffed at that. "I was Mrs. Humphrey Collinwood and I wasn't giving that up without a fight."

She was quiet for a few minutes as the road topped the mountain. Where was she taking him? He had no idea. But he knew how it would end. He could see how agitated she was. She wanted all of this behind her.

"Humphrey loved you like a brother and blamed me for you dropping out of his life," she said, shifting the pickup into four-wheel low as the road became more rocky and rough, the trees more sparse. "He saw us, Ford. At the wedding."

He had started inside, the bitter taste of regret in his mouth.

"I made sure Humphrey saw what he thought was you practically assaulting me. It worked just as I'd hoped. You couldn't stay in our life, Ford. I needed him dependent on me and no one else. If you'd been around, he would have seen through me so much sooner. He didn't want to believe it, but only the two of us knew the truth. I wasn't ever going to tell him, and you were gone from our lives."

But Humphrey had still tried to contact him several times. Had he seen through Rachel even back then? Or had he needed Ford to tell him the truth? Ford realized if he had, he might have saved the man's life.

As Hitch reached the top of the mountain, the pines seemed to open up, but the road still twisted and turned. She was forced to drive slowly over the rocks sticking up in the road. Each corner she came around, she feared she would suddenly come up on the pickup stopped in the road and have no time to react.

It was a relief when the trees opened up even more

and she could see farther ahead. She came around the edge of a wall of rock and suddenly there was the back of the pickup. It appeared to be parked at the edge of the rocky peak. Beyond it, there was nothing but blue sky and empty air.

In that split second, she knew. Ford must have told Rachel what he'd been doing when he'd gotten her call. Hitch hit her brakes and quickly backed up so her SUV was hidden from view. She killed the engine and, grabbing her gun, jumped out. As she neared the pickup and the edge of the mountain, the wind howled, bending the branches of the pines. No wonder they hadn't heard her driving up the mountain behind them, she thought.

She moved quickly, staying at the edge of the trees as she kept her gaze on the two in the pickup. Rachel was behind the wheel—just as Hitch had suspected. Ford appeared to be half slumped in the passenger-side seat. For a moment, she feared he was dead. But Rachel seemed to be talking to him.

As Hitch drew closer, though, her heart dropped when she saw how close Rachel had parked from the edge of a cliff. The engine was still running. Hitch's stomach dropped as she realized what the woman planned to do.

Chapter Twenty-Six

Ford couldn't feel his body. His mind, though, was sharp, and there was nothing wrong with his hearing. He tried not to think about what was going to happen or why living now meant so much to him. Hitch. They'd only just started, and now…

"I didn't want it to end this way, but you have to admit, you gave me the perfect way to get rid of you." Rachel chuckled. "If you hadn't told me about how I'd saved your life with my phone call… Well, I would have found another way, but you did make this easy. I appreciate that."

He made a sound deep in his throat as he looked out at the endless sky. He couldn't see how far it was to the bottom, which was just as well, he thought.

"The thing is, I can't trust you, Ford. If I thought you'd come back for the trial and tell them how much I loved Humphrey and how much he loved me and just keep it to the phone call… But you couldn't do that, could you? You kept digging. Just like that medical examiner. Once Humphrey found my birth control pills, he wouldn't listen to reason. Maybe I wanted him to find them. Maybe I just wanted it all to be over." She sighed.

"You brought this on yourself," Rachel said, as if

working herself up to what she had to do. "You should have just told the sheriff what you'd heard and gone back to Big Sky until the trial. Instead, you got involved with that…woman." Her voice was rising. "You slept with her, didn't you. I saw the way you looked at me after that." He heard the jealousy, saw it in her blue eyes. "You betrayed me. You were the one person I thought I could trust. I trusted you with my life, Ford!" She looked at him as if she hated him. Her laugh was brittle. "She was just using you, and look where it's gotten you."

Rachel took a breath and seemed resolved. "Shyla will be driving up here soon to pick me up. Don't worry. She's coming from another road, so she won't see her husband. That marriage would have never lasted anyway. It's time to say goodbye, Ford."

He said nothing. Even if he could have spoken, he wouldn't have known what to say to someone so cold and calculating, so inherently evil.

Ford watched her as she picked up the winter scraper he kept in his truck to clean ice off the windshield in the winter. She leaned down and jammed it against the gas pedal. The pickup's engine roared. She pried the other end of the scraper against the back of the brake pedal.

This was it, Ford thought, wishing the drug she'd injected him with had knocked him out—not left him in this state where he could see and hear what was happening to him. But he figured Rachel had known what dosage to give him so he would at least mentally suffer until the end. Probably just as she had Humphrey.

As he looked at the drop-off in front of the pickup, he knew he would never have taken this way out. He would have stopped before the end of the road even if Rachel hadn't called.

What had saved his life, though, wasn't Rachel but Hitch. He was falling in love with her, which made dying now so much more painful. He desperately wanted to live to see where this relationship took the two of them. He knew she would be his last thought before the end.

Rachel looked over at him, the engine a roar, so she had to yell to be heard. "I'm sorry it had to end like this." He wondered if she'd said the same thing before she killed his best friend. She reached over and unsnapped his seat belt. Then she shoved the pickup into gear and reached for the door handle as the truck leaped forward.

KEEPING LOW, Hitch crept up the passenger side of the pickup. There had to be a reason Ford hadn't moved, hadn't tried to stop this. She thought about Humphrey. Ketamine. Rachel knew how quickly it worked—and how just as fast it left the body, leaving no trace. If she'd used it on her husband, then why not Ford?

All she knew for sure was that she would get only one chance to pull Ford from the pickup as she heard the engine rev and Rachel struggling to get the sprung driver's-side door open.

Hitch moved fast the moment she heard the engine rev up. She knew she'd have only one chance. She grabbed the passenger-side door handle and yanked it open. As she did, she saw Rachel turn in her direction as she struggled to get out of the driver's-side door.

It all happened in an instant and yet time seemed to stop in that moment, suspended as if frozen. Rachel's expression was one of surprise, then realization as Hitch reached over to unsnap Ford's seat belt and practically throw him from the moving vehicle. Rachel was still struggling to get out, her mouth a perfect O, mimicking the saucer shape of her blue eyes.

Hitch fell from the pickup with her arms wrapped around Ford. She hit the ground hard, knocking the air from her lungs but not breaking her hold on him. She felt the back tire skim past them, felt the edge of the earth so close that one of her feet dangled over the precipice. For a moment, she wasn't even sure that they wouldn't still go over the edge of the cliff after the pickup.

Over the sound of the howling wind, the roar of the pickup's engine, came Rachel's screams. They seemed to go on forever, diminishing as she fell, until the cries finally stopped just moments before the boom of an explosion. The sky below the cliff turned orange and then black with smoke as Hitch dragged herself back from the precipice to stand.

Ford lay on his back staring up at the sky overhead. For a moment, she thought he was dead. But then he blinked. She saw his fingers move. She smiled down at him, then bent and kissed his lips. She felt them move under her own. Pulling back, she brushed his hair from his face as she picked up another sound. Sirens.

Chapter Twenty-Seven

Ford drove through the gateway opening between the mountain and into the Gallatin Canyon. He felt something release inside him as if he was finally coming home. He reached over to squeeze Hitch's hand. Her fresh scent mixed with the smell of new leather. He'd thought he would miss his old pickup when he'd had to replace it. But he'd been wrong about that. He seldom gave that truck a thought.

Anyway, the new-leather smell wouldn't last long, once he went to work on the ranch hauling hay and critters. He couldn't wait.

It was one of those cloudless Montana late-summer days, the sky overhead a bottomless blue. The afternoon sun shone on the pines and the rock rims over the sparkling clear green of the Gallatin River as it wound through the narrow canyon, the mountains rising high on each side. After everything he'd been through, he felt as if he was seeing it for the first time. It was the most beautiful sight he'd ever seen.

He glanced over at Hitch. "You sure you're ready for this?" he asked, grinning. He'd been waiting what seemed like a very long time to take her home to meet his family. The investigation had taken a while to complete even with his testimony about Rachel's confession—and the evidence Hitch had accumulated.

Shyla had been shocked to hear about her husband's death—and maybe even more shocked to find out that he'd been Rachel's accomplice. She had driven up the mountain road at her friend's request with Rachel's suitcases in her trunk. It had seemed a strange request. She'd thought she was taking Rachel to the airport. Little did she know that her best friend never planned for her to leave that mountain alive.

The story all came out over the months that followed. It had been the little things that Rachel had overlooked. All together, though, they painted a picture of a woman desperate to keep her level of living and at the same time get rid of her husband.

In the end, Hitch had put together enough evidence that the investigators almost didn't need his testimony about Rachel's confession. He tried not to think about her and the lives she'd wasted—her own included.

"Meeting your family can't be that scary," Hitch said now with a laugh. "Sounds like there are a lot of them?"

"Between the Cardwells and the Savages, uh-huh. My aunt Dana will insist on throwing a party to get everyone together. It's what she does. She's the matriarch of the family. Everyone pretty much does what she tells them to—even my uncle Hud. Then there is my father and stepmother and all my uncles involved in the Texas barbecue business and my aunts and my cousins…"

"I get the picture," she said with a shake of her head. "You've told them about me? About us? About what I do for a living?"

He nodded. "There are a few cops in the family and

private detectives, and of course Uncle Hud is still marshal, although he's supposed to be retiring."

"Then I should feel right at home," she said, smiling.

"I hope so." He knew they would love her as much as he did. The woman had saved his life. If his aunt Dana had anything to do with it, they would welcome her with a brass band.

HITCH COULDN'T BELIEVE what they'd both been through together in such a short time as she looked out at the gorgeous summer day. It was hard to put it all behind her. She knew it must be even harder for Ford. She could tell coming home was the best medicine for him.

Fortunately, the drug Rachel had injected him with hadn't done any long-term damage. If the near-death experience had brought back his PTSD, it didn't show. He seemed to have come through it stronger and with fewer scars. He credited her with that, but he was strong and he was finding his footing on Cardwell Ranch. Ranching suited him. She loved seeing him happy.

But the fact that she'd almost lost him was never far from her mind. Rachel had proved to be more cold-blooded than even some of the worst male criminals Hitch had run across.

"The sad part," Ford had told her after it was all over, "is that I knew Humphrey. He wouldn't have divorced Rachel and left her penniless, no matter what the prenuptial agreement said. Even with all the lies she'd told him, he still loved her. He would have given her more money than she deserved."

"Not enough for her, though," Hitch had said. "She wanted it all."

"From what she told me, she knew that Humphrey loved her right up to the end. She seemed angry that he still did even when she shot him."

Hitch had wanted Rachel Collinwood to spend her life behind bars. She didn't even deserve a not-very-quick death. But often people didn't get what they deserved.

That thought made her smile, because a part of her thought she probably didn't deserve a man like Ford Cardwell, but she had Rachel to thank for bringing them together. Hitch had fallen in love with him, something that still surprised her, since she'd thought she'd never meet anyone like him.

"Brace yourself," he said now as he slowed the pickup after taking the turnoff to Big Sky. "I can't wait for you to meet everyone. It's just that they can be a bit overwhelming. Also, since I've never brought anyone home before, they're going to know I'm serious about you. Especially my aunt Dana. She'll spot how crazy I am about you right away. She'll be delighted and unable not to show it and get that wedding gleam in her eye. Then there is Uncle Hud—"

"The marshal." Ford drove over the bridge spanning the river. Ahead, she could see the ranch. To her surprise, she actually felt butterflies.

"Hud will be happy to have another person in law enforcement in the family. Not to mention my father. He's been worrying about what I plan to do with my life. He'll think this has happened too fast—"

"It probably has," she said.

He shook his head and smiled at her. "You know when it's right from the moment you feel it."

She nodded as he turned in front of a large two-story house. People instantly began to pour out onto the wide front porch and down the steps. Hitch laughed and couldn't help smiling.

"I wasn't kidding," Ford said. "Want to run now?"

Hitch shook her head. "Nope. You know me. I'm in it for the long haul."

"That's what I'm counting on," he said, and the two of them opened their doors and their arms to his family.

* * * * *

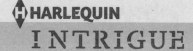
#2007 SAFEGUARDING THE SURROGATE
Mercy Ridge Lawmen • by Delores Fossen

Rancher Kara Holland's hot on the trail of a murderer who's been killing surrogates—like she was for her ill sister. But when Kara's trap goes terribly wrong, she's thrust headlong into the killer's crosshairs...along with her sister's widower, Deputy Daniel Logan.

#2008 THE TRAP
A Kyra and Jake Investigation • by Carol Ericson

When a new copycat killer strikes, Detective Jake McAllister and Kyra Chase race to find the mastermind behind LA's serial murders. Now, to protect the woman he loves, Jake must reveal a crucial secret about Kyra's past—the real reason The Player wants her dead.

#2009 PROFILING A KILLER
Behavioral Analysis Unit • by Nichole Severn

Special Agent Nicholas James knows serial killers. After all, he was practically raised by one and later became a Behavioral Analysis Unit specialist to enact justice. But Dr. Aubrey Flood's sister's murder is his highest-stakes case yet. Can Nicholas ensure Aubrey won't become the next victim?

#2010 UNCOVERING SMALL TOWN SECRETS
The Saving Kelby Creek Series • by Tyler Anne Snell

Detective Foster Lovett is determined to help his neighbor, Millie Dean, find her missing brother. But when Millie suddenly becomes a target, he finds himself facing the most dangerous case of his career...

#2011 K-9 HIDEOUT
A K-9 Alaska Novel • by Elizabeth Heiter

Police handler Tate Emory is thankful that Sabrina Jones saved his trusty K-9 companion, Sitka, but he didn't sign up for national media exposure. That exposure unveils his true identity to the dirty Boston cops he took down...and brings Sabrina's murderous stalker even closer to his target.

#2012 COLD CASE TRUE CRIME
An Unsolved Mystery Book • by Denise N. Wheatley

Samantha Vincent runs a true-crime blog, so when a friend asks her to investigate a murder, she's surprised to find the cops may want the case to go cold. Sam is confident she'll catch the killer when Detective Gregory Harris agrees to help her, but everything changes once she becomes a target...

Desparre, Alaska, was so far off the grid, it wasn't even
listed on most maps. But after two years of running and
hiding, Sabrina Jones felt safe again.

She didn't know quite when it had happened, but
slowly the ever-present anxiety in her chest had eased.
The need to relentlessly scan her surroundings every
morning when she woke, every time she left the house,
had faded, too. She didn't remember exactly when the
nightmares had stopped, but it had been over a month
since she'd jerked upright in the middle of the night,
sweating and certain someone was about to kill her like
they'd killed Dylan.

Sabrina walked to the back of the tiny cabin she'd
rented six months ago, one more hiding place in a series
of endless, out-of-the-way spots. Except this one felt
different.

Opening the sliding-glass door, she stepped outside onto the raised deck and immediately shivered. Even in July, Desparre rarely reached above seventy degrees. In the mornings, it was closer to fifty. But it didn't matter. Not when she could stand here and listen to the birds chirping in the distance and breathe in the crisp, fresh air so different from the exhaust-filled city air she'd inhaled most of her life.

The thick woods behind her cabin seemed to stretch forever, and the isolation had given her the kind of peace none of the other small towns she'd found over the years could match. No one lived within a mile of her in any direction. The unpaved driveway leading up to the cabin was long, the cabin itself well hidden in the woods unless you knew it was there. It was several miles from downtown, and she heard cars passing by periodically, but she rarely saw them.

Here, finally, it felt like she was really alone, no possibility of anyone watching her from a distance, plotting and planning.

Don't miss
K-9 Hideout *by Elizabeth Heiter,*
available July 2021 wherever
Harlequin Intrigue books and ebooks are sold.

Harlequin.com

Get 4 FREE REWARDS!

We'll send you 2 FREE Books <ins>plus</ins> 2 FREE Mystery Gifts.

Harlequin Intrigue books are action-packed stories that will keep you on the edge of your seat. Solve the crime and deliver justice at all costs.

FREE
Value Over
$20

Don't miss the first book in the new and exciting Last Ride, Texas series from *USA TODAY* bestselling author

DELORES FOSSEN

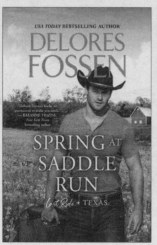

The residents of Last Ride, Texas, which is famous— or more accurately, *infamous*—for its colorful history, have no idea what's about to happen when the terms of Hezzie Parkman's will upend their small-town world...and they discover it's possible to play matchmaker from beyond the grave!

"Clear off space on your keeper shelf, Fossen has arrived."
—Lori Wilde, *New York Times* bestselling author

Order your copy today!

HQNBooks.com